I0526677

Revenge

First Edition

Published by The Nazca Plains Corporation
Las Vegas, Nevada
2008

ISBN: 978-1-934625-60-6

Published by

The Nazca Plains Corporation ®
4640 Paradise Rd, Suite 141
Las Vegas NV 89109-8000

PUBLISHER'S NOTE
Revenge is a work of fiction created wholly by *Christopher Trevor's*
imagination. All characters are fictional and any resemblance to
any persons living or deceased is purely by accident. No portion
of this book reflects any real person or events.

Cover, Les Byerley
Art Director, Blake Stephens

Dedication

To my friend Bob S.
may you get your due

Revenge

First Edition

Christopher Trevor

Contents

INTRODUCTION

In a book I read recently it was said that "Revenge" is a dish best served cold. In the case of this book however, "Revenge" is served up hot, lustfully and heavily. Revenge, also known as vengeance, retribution, or vendetta consists primarily of retaliation against a person or group in response to a perceived wrongdoing. As is the case in the story in this book, "The Abduction of Officer Patrick Curran," written by Steve, wherein a cop who has done his duty in arresting a felon has revenge visited upon him by the felon's buddies. Revenge for the felon and his buddies perhaps, hell for the cop who was simply doing his job. Although many aspects of revenge resemble or echo the concept of justice, revenge usually has a more injurious than harmonious goal. This is outlined superbly in the story "Timmy Gets Revenge...or Does he...hmmm?" written by the recurring character, tickle victim/ hero, Timmy Backman. The goal of revenge usually consists of forcing the perceived wrongdoer to suffer the same pain that was originally inflicted, in this case Timmy making Ronald the tickle victim, or so he thinks...

Revenge, sometimes used in returning the favor-meaning doing something bad to others because they have done something to you-normally bad ethical issue in philosophy or policy, as is told to the hilt in the story 'Squealin' by the dapper and erotic Dutch Roberts.

Some feel that the threat of revenge is necessary to maintain a just society. In this book it seems that revenge against the law and cops prevails. In some societies, it is believed that the punishment in revenge should be more than the original injury, as a punitive measure. In Timmy Backman's story "Revenge of my All Male Staff," a perceived homophobe is dished out revenge right in front of his office staff and contemporaries, and in his CO-worker's perception the homophobe is given the punishment in revenge that he deserves and it surpasses the original injury they believe they have been dealt.

The Old Testament philosophy of "and eye for an eye" tried to moderate the allowed damage, in order to avoid a vendetta or series of violent acts that could spiral out of control-instead of "tenfold" vengeance, there would be a simple equality of suffering. Detractors argue that revenge is a simple logical fallacy, of the same design as "two wrongs make a right." Some state that only God has the moral right to exact revenge, hence the proverb "Vengeance is mine; I will repay, saith the Lord." Indeed, every major religious system contains some method for the mediation of disputes and for the limitation of vengeance by imputing a sense of cosmic justice to replace the often faulty justice systems of the world of men.

So, I invite you to sit down and enjoy this latest book of short stories, this time the subject being "Revenge" and how it is meated out by those who feel they deserve to have it...

Happy Reading,

Christopher Trevor

DEVLIN'S DRUDGE

Written by: Anonymous Cop

Authors note: This story is dedicated to my literary mentor Christopher Trevor who sends me the photos which inspire the tale. Thanks buddy! The bit about the socks at the end was put in just for you.

Captain Josh Devlin was a law unto himself on that long, lonely stretch of road leading out of state. He patrolled it alone, although on rare occasions he allowed some trainee or rookie to ride along with him in order to teach them how "real highway patrol officers" operated. Generally, none wanted to do a second trip with him. It wasn't so much that he was an arrogant, smug, opinionated prick, although those qualities of course played a part, as it was his constant bitching and complaining on just about anything and everything. Devlin never had a good or optimistic word about anything. He hadn't always been that way, of course, but when his wife took the kids and left him flat, his whole personality and demeanor changed and he developed into someone no one liked. And of course the fact that he had seniority and even some political connection (although none of the other officers ever knew exactly what that connection was) made him even more insufferable. But the Captain took most of his personal frustrations out on the truckers who rolled their semis up and down that stretch of highway, transporting their loads from one state to another. Some said that Devlin's wife had run off with a trucker, but no one actually knew if that was true. Nevertheless the Captain made it his personal mission to make life as miserable for the truckers as he could. The long stretch of highway became known as Devlin's Drudge and truckers would often go miles out of their way just to avoid being on it. Others tried to schedule their trips at times when they thought the Captain was off duty but no matter he led the unit in citations given so even though some truckers got through now and then, he eventually caught them. And he knew the regulations and laws inside out and backwards and forward and would be able to spot the minutest violation, be it overweight, speeding, driver not keeping his log book up to date or a myriad of minor rules. And the Captain never once gave a trucker a break. No wonder he was hated.

•————•

Joe Lawton and Mitch Wringer were two long time truckers who had on more than one occasion run afoul of the Highway Patrol Captain and one night over beer at a truck stop café they talked over the problem with a couple of other truckers. It didn't take them long to decide that somehow or other they had to stop this over-zealous cop and show him the error of his ways. They planned and plotted for a couple of weeks and finally came up with what they thought was hopefully the solution.

The Captain was alone, as usual, pulled up off the highway behind a small mound, an area which allowed him clear sight of the highway on both sides but concealed him from the view of vehicles on the road. Devlin was 48 years old but in great shape, despite the beginning of loss of hair and the start of a beer belly which increased with each night's solo drinking in his one bedroom apartment. Say what you want of the man, but his appearance was always top notch with his uniform clean and pressed, his boots highly spit shined, his equipment in perfect working order and his cruiser gassed up, clean and always in perfect condition. He took deep personal pride in his appearance and would jump all over any of the newer recruits who had even a speck of dust on their uniforms. In his own way Captain Devlin was a contented man; well, as content and satisfied as he could be since his ex wife ("the bitch") took the kids and 60 percent of his finances and fled. His contentment came from his job and now he smiled deeply when he spotted the semi rolling down the highway at a good ten miles over the limit. Devlin checked his radar gun just to be sure and noted that the truck was going 79 in a 65 mph zone. Ah yes, he thought, a great way to end my days tour.

He took after the truck, siren wailing, lights flashing and in no time had it pulled over. He made the driver, Mitch Wringer, get down from the cab and present all the necessary paperwork... license, registration, insurance, log book etc. Mitch had been through this before so he said nothing, just did as he was told and stood there grinning at the cop, his Stetson pushed back over his head, his Tony Lemma boots inside his tight fitting jeans, his fingers laced into the heavy leather belt of those jeans.

"What seems to be so funny?" Devlin asked, noticing the grin.

"Oh nothing officer, just thinking what a great day this is."

Devlin looked at the trucker with a puzzled stare but just shrugged and started lecturing him on the posted speed limits. Just at this time another semi came traveling down the road and the officer stopped talking to make note of it. The new semi pulled up behind the first one and the driver got out. This driver was a big man, with powerful arms. He was a guy who obviously worked out at the gym regularly. Devlin stopped talking to the first driver and turned to the second one, with no clue of anticipation that something may be wrong.

"What's the matter buddy, you got problems here?" the cop asked the trucker.

"Oh no officer, I just saw that you were here so I stopped to see if I could be of help."

"Well thanks, but I've got the situation well in hand. I don't need any help," the cop replied.

"Oh you don't understand Cop, it wasn't you I wanted to help, it was my buddy Mitch here."

The Highway Patrolman was a little confused and looked back at the first trucker and just at that moment the trucker let loose with a fist in the cop's stomach which completely knocked the breath out of him. The cop would probably have fallen down from the blow but at the same time the newly arrived trucker wrapped his massive arms around the cop locking him in as tight a hold as the cop had ever imagined. When he kicked his booted legs up and tried to struggle, the trucker just squeezed him all the harder, slowing him down and weakening his efforts.

"You keep fighting me like this copper and I'll break every bone in your chest," the muscular trucker said. "Now be a good boy and relax. Mitch take his gun just to make sure he doesn't pull anything funny."

Mitch approached the helpless cop and took his Glock out of its holster. He also took the cop's cuffs and dangled them before the cop's face. "Maybe we just better cuff up this overgrown pig to save him from having his ribs crushed," he said. Before he could react at all Captain Devlin was tossed to the ground and with one of the truckers holding him down, the other cuffed the hapless cop's wrists behind his back.

The two truckers stood up looking down at the cuffed cop and started laughing at him. "Guess you won't be giving us a ticket today asshole," Mitch said. "But maybe we can give you something. What do you think Joe?"

"I think we should take this ugly shit up behind the hill there and teach him a lesson in respect and humility, that's what I think."

By this time the Captain had his breath back even though he was still gasping from the way Joe had squeezed his lungs. "Listen you morons," he panted, "you're fucking nuts to think you can mess around with a highway patrol officer. You'll get ten years for this shit. Now un-cuff me you jerks."

"Fraid not officer, not yet anyhow. Mitch you lead the cop up behind that hill there and I'll radio Paul that it's clear to come over now." Joe pulled the cop to his feet and reached into his uniform pockets searching for the cruiser's key. "Ah, here's what I want," he said. "After I give Paul the OK, I'll move the cop's car out of sight, just in case. OK pig, get moving." With that Joe gave the cop a slight kick in the ass which had it been harder would have knocked him down again, but it was just enough to get him moving.

Mitch held the cop's weapon against the cop's crotch and said, "Ok copper start walking and don't think I won't blow off your balls if you try anything funny, cause there is nothing I'd rather do."

The poor cop knew that he was in trouble and there wasn't much he could do about it at this time except do what he was told. With Mitch prodding him he walked over the barren land to the hill ahead, wondering the whole time just what the fuck these guys planned on doing to him.

After Joe had radioed Paul, another trucker friend, he started the cop's cruiser and moved it off the highway and behind a knoll where it would be out of sight of any passing traffic, not that any was expected. For some reason he checked the cruiser's trunk and noted some of the cop's equipment, including a Taser gun. Laughing he took the Taser thinking it might be just the thing to get the cop to cooperate faster.

When Joe reached the spot where Mitch and the cop had gone, he found his buddy leaning against a tree smoking a cigar. The cop was kneeling on the ground, his mouth stuffed with what Joe recognized as Mitch's bandana.

"He was bitching and complaining so I had to shut him up," Mitch said. "Telling me how much trouble we were in and what he was gonna do to us when he got free. Only thing I could think of to quiet him down other than shooting him outright." With that both truckers started laughing and the kneeling cop panicked a little and began to sweat. He thought to himself that maybe these fuckers were serious and that he was in more danger than he had first figured.

Joe also lit up a cigar and started talking to the captured cop. "Captain Devlin you are one big son of a bitch and a pain in the ass to all truckers. You go out of your way to harass us causing us to lose time and, more important, money when we have to pay all those dumb fuck fines we get from your tickets. Now it's payback time copper so I hope you're ready for it. What do you think Mitch, should we shoot the bastard or maybe just cut off his balls?"

Mitch laughed, "shit Joe, let's do both."

Just then they heard the sound of another truck pulling up and Joe went down to the highway to welcome his buddy Paul.

Paul Winston didn't look like what a trucker should look like; he was tall, thin and almost nerdy looking, but his looks were deceiving as his wiry strength and iron-willed attitude made him one of the toughest truckers on the road. He was in many ways a jack-of-all trades but today he only had one mission to fulfill – helping in the humiliation and degrading of a "fuckin' cop son-of-a-bitch" who caused a lot of trouble for him and his friends. When he approached his pals he noted the patrolman on his knees, his wrists cuffed behind his back, a red bandana stuffed in his mouth and his face red and sweaty. His two buddies were smoking cigars and leaning against trees. "Well," Paul said, "it looks like that bastard cop is where he belongs, on his knees. I got the camera ready, let's get rolling boys."

•———•

Mitch approached the manacled cop and yanked the bandana from his mouth. The cop started in immediately yelling at the truckers, calling them idiots and assholes and warning them of the trouble they were getting themselves into.

"Shut up pig," Mitch warned.

"No fucking way I'm shutting up you asshole. You're in deep shit so you better undo me now and come to the station with me. I don't know why you lowlifes think you can get away with this because believe me I'm going to..."

That was the last thing Captain Devlin said before Joe fired the Taser into his back; the rest was just screaming. Devlin had used the Taser on a couple of rowdy thugs once and was amazed at how quickly it subdued them. Now he knew why as the electric charge surged through his body sending pain like he never knew existed. He screamed and screamed and begged them to turn it off. He fell face flat on the ground, rolling around in an attempt to ease the pain, all the time screaming and begging them to stop. Joe released the trigger to the Taser and looked down at the groveling cop, his previously perfectly groomed uniform now smudged and covered in dirt.

"Well Captain we'll gladly stop if you just give us a promise that you'll do whatever we say," the muscular trucker growled.

'Yes, yes, anything...only please no more Taser... PLEASE!"

Mitch and Joe just laughed while Paul filmed the whole thing.

"Well copper what do you think you should do for us considering all the problems you've caused in the past? Must be something you can do to make up for that," Joe teased.

"Anything, honest. I won't harass truckers any more I promise. Just let me go, please."

"Well we'll keep you to that promise, but all that is in the future. What about now, what can you do for us now to show you've learned respect?"

Mitch was standing next to the kneeling cop; his legs spread apart, a cigar in his mouth, his hands on his hips. His crotch was even with the face of the bewildered cop.

"I know," he said. "Why don't you give me a blow job?

Show me how sincere you are and that there are no hard feelings. The only "hard feeling" is here in my dick. What do you think copper?"

Captain Devlin was visibly shocked. "What? No way. I'm no fag I don't so that. Hell no, you're crazy. No way."

Mitch moved a little closer to the now sweating cop. He undid the belt holding up his jeans and let them fall to his ankles. Then he pulled his not-yet-completely-hard cock from his boxers and dangled it before the cop. "I think you should suck me off copper," he said.

"No, no...please ...I can't...I don't...I ...oh shit, no please," the cop moaned.

So intent was the cop at trying to avoid looking at Mitch's cock, he never noticed Joe behind him until the muscular trucker wrapped those powerful arms around his chest once again and squeezed. Joe actually lifted the kneeling cop off the ground and placed him squarely in front of his buddy's dangling 8 inch cock.

"Suck it asshole or I'll break every bone in your body and then use the Taser on you again. Do it now!"

The cop's face was shoved directly to the trucker's cock and when the cop opened his mouth to protest again, the trucker shoved the cock into it.

"Now copper I don't want to feel any teeth on my cock. Use your tongue to lick and wet down my tool and then start sucking it in. Do a good job and we'll let you go."

What chance did the poor cuffed cop have but to swallow that cock down his throat? Initially he gagged and sputtered and thought for sure he was going to choke to death but he soon found himself sucking that shaft in and felt it grow even larger inside him. The pressure of Joe's arms squeezing his chest was soon forgotten as the cop sucked and lapped on the cock. He didn't even realize that Joe had released him and that Mitch had his hands on the back of the cop's head and was directing his thrusts and movements as he sucked in earnest. The eruption of warm, sticky cum that exploded inside his throat came as a total surprise to the cop and before he realized what had happened he swallowed most of it. Mitch kept his cock inside the cop's mouth for several minutes after that as it spewed forth after shocks of cum and then slowly settled back to its normal flaccid size. He pulled it out and ordered the cop to lick the remaining cum from the cock head, which the cop did with no argument.

Mitch stepped back, pulled up his jeans and belted them. "Well, copper that wasn't bad at all. You need to practice a lot more but I think you have the basics down. Let's see if you can do a little better with Joe here."

Captain Devlin had his head down, staring at the ground, wondering what was happening to him. When he looked up the muscular trucker was standing there with his pants down, his cock out and a big grin. "Ready when you are cock sucker. But first of all lick these hairy balls of mine, I like that when my bitch does that for me."

And the cop did. He licked and kissed the low hanging balls and even took them one at a time into his mouth. He lapped them hungrily it seemed and drank all the sweat and man grime off them. Then he concentrated all his energy of sucking a cock that was over 10 thick inches. He gagged and struggled for breath but soon had the rhythm going and before long he once again felt the surge of cum as it erupted from the cock head down into his throat. And without being ordered, he licked that head clean when it was removed.

The cop was in a daze at this point, totally confused and unable to understand the emotions and feelings surging through him. He didn't even hesitate when he heard Paul say it was his turn and only vaguely noticed that Paul's cock was much like the man himself, long and slender.

Finally the three truckers were done and felt that the cop had been sufficiently humiliated and abased. Captain Devlin continued to kneel there; his head hung low, his eyes fixed steadily on the ground below. He heard the three truckers laughing at him and acknowledged the fact that they had videotape of the action which would be passed around to other members of the highway patrol if the Captain either reported this or ever again harassed truckers. He just nodded and said he understood and would do what they said.

"Well copper," Mitch was saying, 'I think we understand each other better now. We have to get going, have deadlines to make you know. We'll leave the keys to your cruiser in the ignition; the car is over the next hill on the other side of the highway there. I'm sure you'll find it without any problem." He undid the cuffs from the cop's wrists and dropped them in front of him.

Joe then spoke. "A couple of last minute things copper, just so you won't forget us. The ground from here to your cruiser is pretty rocky so it might be a way of helping you remember this afternoon by doing the walk barefoot. So take off your boots and give them to us; we'll leave them by the cruiser for you."

The cop looked at his captors, puzzled but compliant. He sat up and began pulling off this knee-length leather boots and the heavy black boot socks he wore. When both boots were off, Joe took one of the socks and leaning over stuffed it in the cops mouth; then he used the other sock to tie it in place. The cop didn't try to struggle; he just accepted it.

"Keep that sock in there until you get to your cruiser and don't think we won't be watching somehow and know if you took it out early. You don't obey boy and we come back. Now lay down on your back with your arms by your sides and your legs slightly spread apart."

The cop was still too dazed and confused to try to understand what was happening so he automatically did as ordered.

The three truckers stood over him. Each one unzipped his pants and pulled his cock out and then almost in perfect unison they began to piss all over the prone cop. Piss soaked his tan uniform, splashed in his face, even trickled into his mouth. After releasing their loads on the cop, the truckers left, laughing all the way to their vehicle certain that they no longer had to worry about driving Devlin's Drudge.

Captain Devlin eventually sat up and worked his barefooted way to his vehicle. He feet were cut and bleeding when he got to the cruiser but he didn't bother putting his boots back on; he just removed the spit soaked socks from his mouth and threw them away. He didn't report in after that, just went home and took a long hot shower. The following week he put in his retirement papers and was no longer a Highway Patrolman in a few short days.

•——•

What happened to him, you ask? Well, you can ask him yourself if you want. You can find him every day from 11 a.m. until after 4 p.m. at the men's room glory hole at the truck stop on the interstate. He just can't seem to get enough trucker cum.

SQUEALIN'

Written by: Dutch Roberts

Officers Scott Sepe and David Jackson really hated it when one of their own so easily turned their back on the longstanding regulations the force virtually lived and died by. So, when the two of them got wind that Officer Jeff Michaels might have done just that, they took it upon themselves to get to the bottom of his potentially underhanded ways. The rumors circulating around the station were far too tempting not to want to investigate and confirm them. One juicy claim that stood out – which most simply brushed off as too outrageous – was that Jeff had 'bought' himself a boy toy. What bothered Scott and David the most was that they had already had this nagging suspicion that Jeff did indeed hide a dark mark or two somewhere within his picture perfect record. They were ready to expose him for all it was worth too, growing more than a little tired of his superior attitude. It seemed the entire force was fooled by Jeff's charming 'performance,' as

Scott often referred to it. Ironically, though, these two officers weren't entirely opposed to twisting a few rules of their own to get the answers they needed – just this once, mind you. Scott, in particular, found himself obsessing on a daily basis over bringing the man down.

Sitting in their patrol car, one cold, Sunday afternoon, the two men bantered about what they would do to Officer Michaels once they successfully uncovered his dirty little secrets.

"Damn, I can't wait to see the look on his smug little face when we go to the board with all of the evidence we're sure to uncover" Scott mischievously noted, with an impish grin, just before he took a generous sip of his steaming coffee.

"Yep, it's going to bring the mighty bull to his knees. I can see it now," David confirmed before he took a sip of his own tall coffee, which he cautiously gripped in his oversized, gloved hand.

"You said it, DJ, right to his knees, right where the fucker belongs, begging for us to stop."

"You're really getting into this...or, should I say, getting off on it?"

"Hell yeah, you bet I am. Jeff's going down and we're going to do it. He's had his time to shine, forcing us to take a backseat, calling us out on every little thing we've done wrong along the way. Now it's his turn to eat a little humble pie."

"Don't get cocky, Scott. You know what happens when you get cocky," David cautiously reminded his partner, returning his cup to the holder. "You don't want to do something stupid that he or the force can call you out on."

"Eh, fuck it. This is worth the risk. I mean, honestly, Jeff thinks he can just make off with two million dollars and no one is going to notice or ask any questions? Come on man. Does he really think he's above the law, able to dish out his own judgments as he sees fit? It's time somebody knocked him down a peg or two."

"Yeah, but, remember Scott, no one has been able to pin it on him just yet. If he did have a hand in the disappearance of the money, where did it go? *He* certainly hasn't been enjoying it. Just look at that car he's driving around in. It's a relic. He has to be funneling it through someone else. Maybe he did find himself a boy."

"Well, that's why we need to get to the bottom of this. We need to figure out what role he played, because, damn it DJ, I know he did it. I can feel it man. I can," Scott barked, striking his meaty, gloved fist against the steering wheel before him.

"You're right. You always are," David soothingly noted, attempting to calm his partner of five years.

"That guy at the gym where the money was lost, you know, the owner, Frank, what do you think his angle was?" Scott suddenly and rather randomly blurted out as he adjusted the belt and chest strap on his regulation, leather coat, giving his thickly muscled body room to breathe.

"I don't know. I couldn't get a good read on him. Why? Do you think he was covering something up? Do you think *he's* the rumored 'boy toy'?" David questioned as he too attempted to become more comfortable in his seat, which was always rather difficult for a man of his hulking stature.

"Perhaps," Scott muttered as his dark eyes narrowed and he scanned the highway before them. "Perhaps he was."

Just then, as the two men sat, silently pondering the pieces of the puzzle, watching the light traffic roll by, a red blur whizzed into their line of sight and blazed off in the blink of an eye.

"Shit! Did you see that?" Scott cried out as he reflexively threw the idling patrol car into drive, crushing the gas pedal into the floor with his knee-high leather boot. "They have to be doing an easy 90! What's the radar say?"

"Close, I have 100 even," David barked as he flicked on the overhead lights and siren, "and in a 65 zone too, with construction going on! They're just asking for trouble," he added, attempting to get a read on the plate so he could enter it into their on-board computer.

"Damn, they're flying, man. I'm clocking 110 now," Scott hollered as he inched his way closer, soaring around a white mini-van that gave off the appearance of standing still.

"I've almost got a read on the plate," David informed his partner as his hands flew over the keyboard of the portable computer.

"Shit, look at them go. They're riding this road like a fucking whore in heat," bellowed Scott as he sharply cut the wheel, keeping the sports car in his line of sight.

"Hey, watch your mouth," David reprimanded his partner, regardless of Scott's rank and seniority over him.

The two vehicles roared down the highway, swerving between the few cars that were out for a lazy, afternoon drive. There were several, potentially dangerous moments when one or both of the cars nearly struck the cement divider, however, both drivers managed to maintain control enough to avoid such an incident from happening.

Secretly, Scott had to admit, whoever the lunatic was, they certainly knew how to handle themselves behind the wheel of a sports car and what a beauty it was! If he wasn't mistaken he was trailing a brand-new GranTurismo, which, most likely, cost the driver a huge wad of money, that is, *if* the driver actually owned the striking vehicle.

"Should we call for backup?" David suddenly questioned his partner, continuing to focus on the read he was getting from the computer.

"No, this one is all ours," Scott coolly responded with a focused look on his ruggedly handsome face. "What's the comp say?"

"The driver is one Mark Duncan or, I should say, the car is registered in his name. If it is him behind the wheel, he's a Caucasian male, just turned 24, and it appears that he is the soul owner of the car. However, and you may find this interesting, he also appears to still live at home and is currently unemployed. No priors."

"That is pretty remarkable," Scott spat. "So, how does such a kid afford a set of wheels like that? You did say owner...right? Mommy and daddy didn't buy it for him?"

"Correct," David confirmed, closing the computer down, redirecting his pitch-black eyes to the road ahead. "He's definitely the owner and, I must admit, for a kid, Mr. Duncan can sure handle himself. He's almost as good as you."

"Yeah, well, I wonder how well he'll do behind bars, because at this rate, DJ, he's just asking to be caught and put away."

"Let's not jump to any conclusions, Scott. He may have a very valid reason why he's attempting to break the sound barrier," David mockingly replied as his eyes narrowed in on the flashy, red sports car, which gradually – and finally – seemed to be slowing down. "It may not even be him, but some professional. Although, I didn't see any reports listed for a stolen vehicle of that make and model."

"Well, whoever it is I guess they finally woke up and realized we're here," said Scott, eyeing up the car more closely as he bridged the gap between them.

"Yeah, I guess so. Either that or they have to make a quick pit stop. It looks like they're pulling into the next rest area," David noted, then quickly added, "Wait, isn't that the stop we shut down last week because of the problems in the restroom?"

"Yep," Scott confirmed, pulling off the ramp, whizzing by the clearly posted CLOSED sign. "I think I still have the key to the padlock. Anyway, let's be ready for anything. Someone like this may come off confrontational. Perhaps even a bit violent. I'll be surprised if they cooperate at all. Just remember, let's not act hasty."

"Me? Act hasty? You're the one who was just shipping them off to prison," David evenly noted as they pulled in behind the car, which was most agreeably parking ahead of them.

"When we approach we'll ask the driver to exit the car. I think a sobriety test could be in order," Scott announced as he reached for his regulation hat, placing it squarely upon his head, covering his dark, spiky hair.

"I agree, even if it is just about noon. The driver could be returning home after a late night of heavy drinking. They could still be intoxicated," his partner confirmed as he placed his own hat upon his head, concealing his completely bald scalp that had the appearance of highly polished obsidian marble, which was befitting, since the man's entire body gave off the appearance of smooth, black stone.

"Oh yeah, this one is going down hard. I can feel it," Scott noted with an air of excitement in his voice as he reached to undo his seatbelt.

"Why do I get the sneaky suspicion you're riding on the high you're developing over the possibility of exposing Officer Michaels?"

"What if I am, DJ?"

"Just be careful not to get carried away. Ok? Don't let it consume you. This situation has nothing to do with that one."

"Ok, fine, I hear you loud and clear," Scott reassured his partner as he let his seatbelt go, allowing it to whip back into place.

Stepping from the patrol car, the two officers made their way forward, each taking a side of the vehicle. Their stiff, polished boots clicked upon the pavement in stereo. Officer Sepe made his way toward the driver, while Jackson took up a position outside the passenger side, which – to the best of their knowledge – was vacant. The two men appeared very imposing in their dark-blue uniforms, wide brimmed, Mounties-style hats, leather gloves, boots, and three-quarter length jackets.

Standing with his knee-high boots spread wide, Scott patiently waited for the driver to roll down their slightly tinted window. A twisted part of the officer always perked up in the moment he got to see the expression of the person behind the wheel. He enjoyed having the upper hand in the situation, towering over the person, placing them in the submissive role from the start. What he inwardly loved, as well, was how drivers in sharp, low-to-the-ground sports cars – just like the one before him – received a fantastic view of his fully packed, uniform encased crotch, which nicely dipped out from just below the hem of his coat. What he didn't like was when the roles were reversed and he was caught off guard by the sight of the driver. That, thankfully, rarely ever happened.

Today, however, to the officer's surprise, was one of those exceptional occasions.

As the window slid down, Scott immediately felt his dominance over the situation melting away. Sitting behind the wheel of the car was easily the best-looking driver he had ever seen in the flesh. Hell, the kid was absolutely stunning. The officer's senses were completely overwhelmed – that's how gorgeous the guy was – which caused Scott to take pause, instead of coolly and calmly proceeding. He nearly forgot to breathe as he drank in the driver's strong, square jaw, luminous, tan skin, plump, luscious lips, and glossy, jet-black hair, which spilled in perfectly styled, thick waves down to his broad shoulders.

"Everything ok, Sir?" the driver audaciously asked as he removed his sunglasses, revealing breathtaking eyes the color of sparkling emeralds.

"Officer Sepe, do you require my assistance?" David prompted from the other side of the car, sensing his partner's altered and somewhat shaky disposition.

Snapping back into reality, upon hearing David's deep voice, Scott swiftly attempted to shake off the spell this charming kid was casting over him. Finding his own deep voice once again, he firmly ordered, "Please step out of the car."

"Yes Sir," the kid simply replied, with a winning smile, giving no sign of resistance, however, he boldly inquired, "Do you mind if I grab my coat? It's sort of cold out there."

"That would be a good idea. This may take some time. However, please allow my partner to retrieve it for you," Scott acknowledged, giving the stunning kid space to exit.

"Sure, it's in the backseat. Should I fetch my paperwork now or would you like to get that for me too?"

Thrown back a bit by the overconfidence of the driver, Scott simply replied, "Your license will do. Please step out of the car now. Officer Jackson will retrieve your coat."

"Yes Sir."

Firmly standing his ground, Scott watched as the young, cocky driver proceeded to slide out of the sports car. Caught off guard for a second time, the officer found himself silently gawking at the kid and his very striking attire, which seemed completely out of place for both the setting – a dirty, rundown rest area – and the time of day – a quiet, Sunday afternoon.

It was as if the guy had just walked off of a runway. From head to toe, he was outfitted in the sharpest, most beautifully crafted evening attire Scott had ever seen with his own two eyes. To make matters worse, or better – depending on your point of view – it was painfully obvious the body contained within the exquisite, formal garment was equally stunning and built to perfection.

"Going somewhere special?" Scott found himself asking the raven-haired kid as he took the license that was being offered to him from within a leather-encased paw of a hand.

"My class reunion," the kid coolly replied, shifting his muscular form from one leather dress boot to the other. "It starts in a few hours."

"I see. Must be one heck of a reunion," said Scott, with a sharp tone, as his dark eyes briefly pulled away from the tempting image before him to scan the document in his own gloved hand. It appeared that this kid was indeed Mark Duncan.

"Is there a problem, Sir?"

"Well, it seems a bit...much," Scott began, trying to select his words carefully, as he motioned to Mark's attire, temporarily neglecting the real reason he pulled the kid over. "Don't you think, Mr. Duncan?"

"Not at all," said Mark, redirecting his attention to Officer Jackson who was making his way around the front of the car with an eye-catching top coat in his gloved hand. Taking the thick, full-length, cream-colored, lynx fur from the cop, the tuxedo-clad jock genuinely smiled and added a simple, "Thank you."

Scott watched as Mark slid into the over-the-top, albeit dazzlingly beautiful garment, which, once in place upon his broad shoulders, framed his suited, muscular form perfectly.

"Not at all, huh?" Scott muttered more to himself as he made eye contact with his partner who was also shaking his head at the sight of Mark in his ostentatious clothing.

"Officer Sepe, a moment of your time?" David inquired, motioning to his partner to step to the rear of the car. "This will only take a minute," he added, directing the statement toward Mark, who seemed to be lost in fussing with the polished buttons on his pretty coat. "Certainly, Sir, take your time," was his rather casual reply, as the two officers stepped away.

"You may not believe this, but...I have a feeling we were just handed two million dollars, dressed like Mr. Bond, in a bright red package," David began, once he and Scott were safely out of earshot.

"You're kidding me...right?" replied Scott with wide eyes and raised eyebrows, feeling his body begin to tingle with excitement.

"Check this out," David directed, as he handed his partner a folded piece of paper. "I stumbled upon it when I went to get his rather new and absolutely expensive coat. Take note of the letterhead."

Scott stood with his back to Mark and unfolded the piece of paper. It was a letter from Frank's Gym, confirming Mark's recent separation as an employee. With a knowing grin he unnecessarily pointed out to his partner, "So, it looks like Mr. Duncan once worked for the very same gym Officer Michaels mysteriously lost some money in."

"So it seems," David confirmed with an iniquitous grin of his own.

"I guess that explains how he's able to afford the fancy car and prissy clothes, without a job in sight," said Scott, eyeing Mark up in all his glory, feeling his loins start to stir in response to this exciting development. "Now we just need him to admit that he knows Michaels and that the money came from him."

"Wait," David suddenly blurted, grabbing Scott's bulging arm just as he was making a move to confront Mark. "We can't just grill him on the side of the road. What grounds do we have? I think we need to probe this kid, real deep, and coax the rest out of him as we go along. The more pressure we apply, the sooner he'll crack. He's an inexperienced punk. He'll slip sooner or later. Perhaps divulging a little of what we already know will get him squealing in no time."

"But what if he doesn't? We just write him a few tickets and send him on his way?"

"We'll worry about that when the time comes, Scott. Just keep your cool."

In unison, the two officers turned and made their way back

toward Mark who was now leaning against his car, arms folded over his massive pecs, with a sardonic smile on his full lips.

"I would strongly recommend you wipe that smile off of your face, Mr. Duncan," Scott boldly began, moving as close to Mark as possible without overstepping his bounds. "You're in a good deal of trouble," he firmly added, inhaling the strong, masculine cologne that was wafting off of the sharp dressed kid, gently riding along on the cold, winter breeze.

"I am?" Mark daringly replied, stepping away from his car, with a fresh look of innocence on his attractive face.

"Well, to start, you were driving well above the speed limit."

"I was?" Mark continued to question, playing the ignorance card.

"Yes, 30 to 35 miles over the limit, if I'm not mistaken, in a construction zone. You weren't aware of this?" Scott tightly replied, biting his tongue to the best of his ability, wanting so desperately to knock the smug look off of Mark's perfect face.

"Sorry, no, I wasn't aware I was going that fast, Sir. It's a new car. I guess I still need a bit more time behind the wheel," said Mark with a shrug of his broad shoulders, moving back toward the sleek vehicle.

"See, Officer Sepe, I told you he had a valid reason for speeding," David interjected. "It's a new car. He's still trying to get a feel for how she handles."

"Right...a new car," Scott quipped, flexing his thick fingers inside of his gloves, feeling his manhood begin to stiffen inside of his tight pants as his body became even more charged over the effortless capture of such a magnificent trophy. Officer Michaels' downfall was swiftly on its way to becoming a reality. It was almost too good to be true.

"Brand new," Mark confirmed, running his own gloved hand over the gleaming, silver door handle.

"If I can be so *frank* as to ask...how much do one of these run?" Scott questioned, joining Mark by the shining vehicle, allowing the smooth sleeve of his regulation, leather coat to brush against the thick sleeve of Mark's luxurious fur coat.

"Well, uh...a very pretty penny," Mark suddenly sputtered, starting to lose his cool under the steady, intense gaze of the officer who was now standing a little too close for comfort.

"Ok, I figured that much, but, come on, spill...what did this baby really run you?" Scott continued to pry, feeling Mark's defenses being to slip away.

"I'm not sure this question is all that relevant to the situation, Sir," Mark swiftly replied, regaining an ounce of his previous cool demeanor as he shifted in his dress boots, attempting to put some distance between himself and Scott.

"Well, you may not feel it is, but we certainly do. Don't we, Officer Jackson?" Scott prompted his partner, shifting his colossal body to match Mark's every move.

"Correct, Officer Sepe, I believe it is *very* relevant to the situation," David confirmed as he relocated his own massive form to the opposite side of Mark, confining the kid between two rock-solid pillars of uniformed muscle.

"How so?" Mark brazenly questioned the advancing officer, regaining a bit of his cocky attitude, regardless of his somewhat awkward positioning between the two hulking men.

"Well, Mr. Duncan, you may not be aware of this, but the local authorities, in particular, the two officers standing before you, are searching for a suspect who made off with a rather large sum of money that didn't belong to them."

"Oh?" Mark cautiously replied, self-consciously running a gloved finger along the stiff collar to his dress shirt, which suddenly looked rather tight around his thick, muscular neck.

"We have reason to believe that this person has foolishly decided to remain in the area and, get this, they carelessly gave some of the money away, allowing someone else to spend it on extravagant items. For example, a new car," Scott matter-of-factly noted, while running a steady hand over the sports car before them, without batting an eyelash.

"And, perhaps, a new wardrobe too," David added, giving Mark a wry look. "Nice coat, by the way."

"Uh, thanks...," Mark muttered, feeling his world close in around him, suddenly losing his cocky edge as he nervously ran a hand over one of the wide lapels of his coat.

'You wouldn't happen to know anything about such a person? Would you Mr. Duncan?" questioned Scott, giving the kid the perfect opportunity to squeal on Officer Michaels.

"Uh, no, I wouldn't," Mark bravely sputtered without hesitation, holding his ground as best he could.

"Hmm, that's a shame, because, to be honest, we're not really looking to bring down the person running around spending the money. Not yet. But, we're definitely looking to capture the person who took the money in the first place. Although, it'd be great if the one blowing the cash got wind of our situation, I bet they would turn their partner over to us in a heartbeat. You know, not wanting to lose their share of the takings and all."

"Probably," Mark whispered now as a bead of sweat formed on his upper lip.

"Hmm, are you feeling ok, Mr. Duncan?" David inquired, sensing the kid's edginess. "You don't look so good."

"No...I'm fine," Mark muttered, glancing from one officer to the other, scrambling to hold it together.

"Are you sure?" Scott prodded, shifting his body closer, feeling his rigid manhood run along the inside of his left thigh.

"I, uh...I could do with a run to the bathroom. If that's ok with the two of you," Mark sincerely asked, eyeing up the nearby facility, suddenly looking more desperate than devastatingly handsome.

"It's closed. Didn't you see the sign?" said David, glancing to his partner, subtly motioning for him to withhold the information that they had the key to get in.

"Oh, no, I guess I didn't," Mark muttered, shifting his weight from one foot to the other as he felt his cock stiffen within his tailored pants with the burning need to unload a long, hot piss.

"Well, that's a shame. I guess you'll have to hold it in until we get back to the station," Scott casually informed Mark, getting a rise out of the kid's swiftly changing facial expressions.

"What?!" the kid exclaimed in return, with a look of utter shock on his handsome face.

"Well, at this point, I think we need to impound this car and then we'll revoke your license," Scott continued to inform Mark, feeling his cock buck within his pants at the sheer excitement of toying with the kid. "Unless you can come up with a reason why we shouldn't go ahead and do just that. I mean, if you could help us out in any way with our situation, we just may be able to overlook your infractions here today. I mean, you had to have run into someone suspicious looking when you purchased this flashy car...or this pretty coat. They were probably out shopping right alongside you."

Mark stood, silently, thinking the situation over. The officers could almost see the wheels turning, smell the smoke burning.

"Mr. Duncan?" David prompted the kid, wondering if he was on the edge of finally breaking. "What's it going to be? Something tells me you wouldn't want to find yourself behind bars."

"I could go to jail for speeding?" Mark sputtered with a wild look in his eyes.

"Hmm, not for speeding, but you could easily serve time for say...reckless driving, or evading the law perhaps. Maybe even indecent exposure in a public place," Scott chimed in with a wicked grin as he casually shifted his body, giving his energized cock room to stir in his pants.

"Indecent exposure?" Mark spat, looking to David for an explanation, completely confused by this announcement.

Shrugging, David had nothing to offer the kid, since he wasn't all that sure himself where his partner was going with this false accusation, yet, he was all too willing to play along. There was something entertaining about fooling around with this kid.

"Well, you know, being that the restrooms are closed, wouldn't it seem reasonable that we would come upon Mr. Duncan relieving himself right here in the parking lot?" Scott informed his partner.

"I guess so," David concurred, nodding his head in agreement, "or perhaps we caught him fooling around. He is dressed a little like a male prostitute and we have had some issues with this particular rest area."

"But...I...you can't accuse me of something I didn't do," Mark cried, choosing to ignore the derogatory comment about his choice of clothing, focusing more on his need to piss. He could feel his cock painfully throbbing with the overwhelming build-up churning inside of his full bladder. They needed to move this along or he was going to piss himself.

"Well, you didn't expose yourself just yet, but I have feeling you are about ready to," said Scott, moving closer to Mark. "Or do you plan on soiling your fancy new clothes?"

As Mark pondered this question, Scott and David calmly waited, each one wondering if they were going to have to push him even harder to get the answers they so desperately needed. Scott, however, found himself swiftly losing his patience with the kid, so much so, that he almost told his partner to go wait in the patrol car so that he could handle this situation his way, which wasn't going to be pretty – legal, but not pretty. Well, at least he hoped he would be able to keep things on the up and up.

"So? What's your answer, Mr. Duncan?" David evenly questioned the kid.

Mark remained broodingly silent, which only aggravated Scott even more.

"That's it. I've had it," he suddenly barked. "Officer Jackson, go wait in the patrol car," he commanded, pulling rank on his partner, choosing to go with his gut reaction to this situation.

Confused by this turn of events, both Mark and David stood looking at one another with perplexed expressions on their faces, unable to take action quick enough.

"Officer Jackson, I gave you an order. Now go," Scott spat. "You," he then barked at Mark, with a stiff, leather-clad finger directed at him, "are coming with me."

Calmly turning his back on the situation, David made his way toward their vehicle, swiftly abandoning Mark to his own devices. He knew he should have made an attempt to reason with his partner, but after five years out in the field with him, he knew better. In an odd, twisted sort of way, he completely trusted Scott, regardless of how he handled things. Besides, the kid had this coming to him...didn't he?

Waiting no more than a split second after his partner's departure, Scott firmly shoved Mark toward the deserted restrooms. "Get moving, pretty boy," he barked at the kid, abandoning all protocols.

Mark, slightly confused by this command, awkwardly made his way toward the closed facility. Well, at least he had been informed that it was shut down, however, by the way Officer Sepe was moving him along, something told Mark this wasn't necessarily the truth.

Standing before the padlocked door to the restroom, Mark suddenly was reminded just how bad he needed to pee. His throbbing cock, which was rock hard with piss, twitched a bit inside of his pants, urging him to quickly take care of business. What was ironic was how Scott's cock mirrored Mark's in its painful, throbbing state, but his was for a completely different reason. His cock was aching to be relieved of the hot seed, which was boiling inside of his full sac, waiting to be spewed in honor of the exhilarating capture of Mark and, soon enough, Jeff.

Taking the key from his wide utility belt, Scott swiftly undid the lock and directed Mark inside, subtly adjusting the crotch of his pants as he brought up the rear.

As they entered the enclosed space, it was overpoweringly obvious that the facility had been abandoned in a state of utter filth and disrepair. Immediately Mark's delicious cologne was engulfed by the foul stench of fecal matter, as well as several other pungent and repulsive odors. Gagging and gasping for fresh air, Mark staggered back a bit, nearly knocking Scott over.

"Where do you think you're going?" asked Scott, blocking Mark's only route out of the disgusting place with his broad, muscular form. "You said you needed to use the restroom. Well, here we are. Use it!"

Flicking on the stark, cold overhead lights, Scott presented to Mark the full, nauseating picture of what was once – a very long time ago – a pristine, public restroom. To the tuxedo-clad jock, it appeared that the room recently suffered from some serious plumbing issues. There were brown and yellow smears and stains, as well as murky puddles everywhere – on the walls, the floor, even the ceiling. To the officer, it was a crime scene, the result of an out-of-control, doped-up gang, hell bent on destroying the facility, just for the sheer amusement of doing it.

Mark looked to Scott and silently pleaded with his bright eyes.

"What? Don't have to go anymore?" Scott questioned, crossing his thick, leather encased arms over his full chest, enjoying the sight of the impeccably dressed, muscle stud, standing in the middle of absolute squalor.

Mark shook his head.

"Well, tough, because we're not leaving until you do," Scott informed the kid. "Unless you have something you need to share with me?"

Mark, overwhelmed by the stench, began to gag again. His eyes even began to water; however, it was in this moment, between fits of coughing, that the crisp, clearly defined outline of Scott's raging cock was finally acknowledged. Scott could see it register, as Mark's emerald eyes went wide and his succulent mouth went a bit slack.

"You...you brought me here to...," Mark sputtered, gesturing to the officer's fully packed pants.

"I'm not sure what you're carrying on about, Mr. Duncan," replied Scott, pretending to be unaware of his pulsating package. "Are you going to utilize the facilities or not? If not, we will join Officer Jackson back in the patrol car and head off to the station to process your arrest. If so, then I suggest you get moving."

"No...I...," Mark muttered, fussing a bit with the buttons on his thick top coat.

"Christ, kid, what's it going to be? I don't have all day. I've given you your options, now decide, before I do it for you!" Scott barked, his voice reverberating off of the dirty tiled walls, cutting through Mark. "I mean, shit or get off the pot already."

Once again, Mark stood ramrod still and tightlipped, attempting to forget about the fact that he had to take a wicked piss.

"You know what? I think it's time to show you how one of my fellow officers would handle this situation. I warn you, it's not going to be pretty," Scott promised. "By the way, refer to me as Officer Michaels from now on or I'll fucking cut your balls off and feed them to you! That's the man I'm going to impersonate. Perhaps my performance will jar your memory. He's a really great guy. I hope I'll be able to do him some justice."

Without another twisted, threatening word, Scott

advanced on Mark, a conflicting mix of anger and lust playing over his face as he approached. With his smooth, leather encased hands he swiftly reached out and took a hold of the thick, wide lapels to Mark's luxurious coat. Stretching his powerful arms wide, Scott instantly split the front of the substantial garment open, sending several of the polished buttons flying through the sour air. Continuing to yank on the wide lapels, Scott tugged and pulled, until the stitches holding them in place started to snap. In an instant, with very little resistance, they started to come free from the body of the coat.

SNAP!

SNAP!

RIP!

"Do you think you're something special, boy?" the enraged officer spit, yanking his clenched fists downward, continuing to render the once stunning lapels obsolete, all the while, drawing the dumbfounded kid's muscular form closer to his own uniformed physique.

Gasping and groaning, Mark swiftly found himself eye to eye with Scott, their bodies firmly pressed against one another. The man's hot, raw breath washed over his face, causing his cheeks to flush. With his coat splayed open, Mark could easily feel his own rigid cock being smashed up against that of the officer's, both straining against the thin fabric of their respective pants. Within a heartbeat, his sensual, thick lips were meeting the same fate – nearly devoured by Scott's hungry, warm mouth, after being nibbled and brutally mashed.

Drawing back, Scott proceeded to spit a massive wad directly into Mark's face, followed by him howling, "Huh, you don't taste like anything special. Let me try again." Leaning in, he proceeded to run his tongue over Mark's cheek, nose, and brow, slurping in the spittle he splattered there.

Thrusting his hips, Scott continued to grind his throbbing crotch into Mark's, until suddenly, he felt exactly what he was hoping for – a damp, piss-warm mound. He had struck the kid's crotch just so and with enough force, it drove Mark to wet himself.

"Aw, boy, have you made a mess of your pretty tux?" Scott wickedly questioned the ill-looking kid.

Stunned silence was the reply given, that and the sound of the hot piss dripping upon Mark's dress boots, which had quickly made its way down his powerful, muscular legs, flowing like a river from his thick cock.

"I asked you a question, boy!" Scott boomed, letting spittle fly from his mouth and rain down upon Mark's perfectly tied bow tie.

"Uh...yes," Mark meekly replied, feeling ashamed and horrified over pissing himself.

"Yes...what?"

"Yes...Sir?"

"NO!" Scott hollered, swiftly reaching for a pocket on Mark's coat and rending it open with one hard jerk of his gloved hand, sending the car keys found within clattering to the floor.

RIP!

"Yes...Officer Michaels?"

"Correct," said Scott, ripping the pocket, along with its silk lining, completely off. "That's a good boy. To be honest, I didn't think you had it in you."

Mark, still freely relieving himself, allowing a puddle to form around his feet, began to wonder how long this torture would go on and, more importantly, if he would make it out in one piece. It was obvious his exquisite clothing wasn't going to be that lucky. His pride was yet another potential casualty.

"Now, I need to understand why you think you can get away with driving and dressing like you do," Scott continued, with a sneer on his lips. "You are far too young to think you're somebody who can get away with such behavior. No one is that cocky at your age. I don't care who you are or who you know," he paused, then snidely inquired, "Do you know anyone special, boy?"

Mark remained silent, allowing the officer to ramble on with his horrible impression of Jeff.

"I didn't think so," Scott spat and then continued. "You know what? You remind me of all of those fucking pretty boys back in high school who thought their shit didn't stink. You know the ones – all talk and no action. I couldn't stand them then and I can't stand them now. I won't tolerate such behavior in my presence. Trust me, boy, your shit stinks real bad and you're going to get a good taste of it!"

Swiftly, Scott firmly took a hold of Mark by the thick collar of his coat and proceeded to drag him to the row of filthy, piss stained urinals. Catching the kid off guard, he sucker punched him and then quickly took advantage of his weakened, slightly bent posture. Pulling Mark erect by his thick, wavy hair, he forced him face-first against the tiled wall, allowing his hip to smash into the solid urinal before him. The officer then moved into position behind him, pinning him into place with a knee to his lower back, forcing his damp crotch against the latrine. Grabbing Mark's left arm, Scott skillfully whipped a pair of silver cuffs onto his wrist and then immediately shackled him to the nearest rust encrusted flusher. Within seconds he had his right arm extended and cuffed the very same way. In a matter of minutes, Officer Sepe had Mark · spread-eagle and chained in place.

"Damn, boy, you didn't put up much of a fight. It's almost like you want this to happen," observed Scott, feeling his cock jolt in his pants, which only reminded him of how hot and bothered he was becoming over this whole situation.

Jeff was going down and, as a bonus, so was his money hungry, boy toy!

Stepping behind Mark, Scott leaned in and whispered into his ear, "Do you cry out when you get fucked in the ass or are you the strong silent type?"

Mark instantly tensed up, dreading what was about to come next, but he had already decided he would do whatever it took to keep Jeff out of this. If he was going down, he was going down alone.

"Bring it on...fucker," Mark found himself muttering through clenched teeth.

Incensed by this nasty reply, the aggressive officer was more than happy to oblige the kid. Bending down and taking the hem of Mark's fur coat into his gloved hands, Scott violently tore the once gorgeous garment right up the middle, splitting the creamy, soft body of the coat, as well as the smooth, silk lining into two halves from vent to collar. By doing this, he soon exposed the impeccably tailored tuxedo found within. In a flash, the tuxedo jacket, with its already generous vent and silky, rich lining, was being torn from hem to neck as well, exposing the pristine white layer of Mark's crisp, form-fitted dress shirt, which was neatly tucked into the satin waistband of his sleek pants. Groping at this glossy band, Scott quickly found the tightly stitched, vertical seam – which the officer imagined lined up perfectly with Mark's ass crack – and, tugging on it with all his strength, managed to split it in two as well.

"Almost there," Scott muttered, giving the split seam another violent, nasty tug, rending it open in a flash.

RIP!

Soon enough Mark's sexy, silk boxers were in plain sight as Scott tore at the tailored pants, splitting them open, letting them drop from the kid's narrow waist and pool around his sheer sock encased ankles and leather encased feet.

"Oh, fuck, just look at that firm ass!" Scott howled, lifting the tail to Mark's dress shirt, running a gloved hand over the two full, perfectly shaped, muscular mounds held within the smooth fabric. "Something tells me your ass has barely been explored."

Attempting to remain uncooperative, Mark simply grunted with each assault on his clothing and body. Inwardly he was repulsed and disgusted, but on the surface he appeared completely detached. He knew what had to be done.

Stepping close to the bound kid once more, Scott took a hold of the splayed layers, which were loosely hanging, and violently tore them wider; forcing the tattered halves to bunch up on Mark's extended, well-developed arms, completely separating them at the collar. As he did this he could hear the buttons that ran down the front of the tuxedo jacket snap and simply clatter into the porcelain urinal set before the kid.

PLINK!

PLINK!

PLINK!

Smiling, Scott swiftly undid the silver clasp holding Mark's silk, pleated cummerbund in place. Whipping it from around his narrow waist, the officer fondled the handsome accessory for a few seconds, admiring the craftsmanship. Then, without warning, he took the midnight-colored sash and worked it into a gag, placing it neatly over Mark's mouth, tightly tying it off at the back of his head, forcing his mouth into a maniacal, gaping grin.

"There we go, boy, it doesn't matter if you're a vocal fuck or not," Scott evenly noted. "No one will be able to hear you now. It's not like you had much to say to begin with, which, to be honest, really didn't help your case very much."

Tracing his gloved hands down Mark's broad back, the officer proceeded with the crisp, pressed dress shirt still neatly in place upon his v-shaped torso, giving it the same treatment as the coat and jacket. Taking a utility knife from his belt, Scott made a quick cut at the hem of the shirt, just above Mark's ass. After returning the knife to its rightful place, the officer grasped the two sides of the once flawless fabric and slowly began to split it up toward the stiff collar found at Mark's neck. Inch by inch, smooth, rippling muscles were revealed. Thick and perfectly formed, the kid's backside was a work of art. Every curve, every cut, every last inch was stunning. No wonder Officer Michaels was so willing to break the law and hand over the money to this stud. Scott would have probably done the same thing – if given the chance. This kid was that tempting.

Finishing the split just below the collar, Scott took the time to leave the stiff, white band, as well as the dark, silk bow tie in place. He simply tugged on the thin fabric until it came free from the collar. Yanking on the material that formed the shoulders and sleeves, he let them join the rest of the tattered chunks on Mark's extended arms. As he did this, he could hear the diamond studs falling from their place down the front of the dress shirt, joining the buttons from the kid's jacket in the bottom of the urinal.

PLINK!

PLINK!

PLINK!

PLINK!

Taking a step back, Scott surveyed his handiwork. With the exception of Mark's prissy, black, silk boxers, he nearly had the kid ready for one hell of a deep fisting and fucking. Glancing down at his throbbing package, he could see a dark, wet stain forming on the fabric of his crotch. He needed to release the load in his balls before he wasted it and exploded inside of his pants. Giving it over to this stud was the perfect solution.

Undoing his thick, rather heavy utility belt, Scott casually let it drop to the piss stained floor below. He allowed it to clatter and clank, signaling to the kid that the moment had come for his ass to be taken. Stripping off his thick leather coat, the officer quickly moved on to the clasp and zipper found on his pants. Undoing them and allowing them to slide down, he revealed not only his jockstrap encased manhood, but his beefy, lightly haired buttocks in all their glory.

Mark could sense Scott approaching. He could hear his boots shuffling upon the debris littered floor, inching their way closer. He began to feel the man's hot breath on his exposed back. The fucker was coming and what was about to happen wasn't going to be pretty. The man had promised Mark that. He couldn't help but wonder where the hell Jeff was when he needed him the most. Clenching his rock-hard ass muscles, Mark drew in a deep breath, focused on the dirty, tiled wall before him, and waited for the assault to happen.

And waited.

And waited.

Quickly, he realized something was wrong, as he heard a sudden scuffle directly behind him.

Attempting to see what was going on, Mark struggled in his restraints. As he turned to look for Officer Sepe, his eyes fell upon a far more exhilarating and hopeful sight. Not only was the crazed officer behind him, with his pants down around his knees, but there, without warning, was Officer Jeff Michaels, in all his uniformed glory!

The two husky men struggled for dominance in the situation and, thankfully, Jeff swiftly came out on top, utilizing the element of surprise to his advantage. In a flash he had Scott pinned, face first, in a puddle of urine. He then yelled up to Mark, "Keep your eyes forward! You didn't see or hear any of this! Got it?"

Mark did as he was told, yet, he couldn't help but feel the giddy need to watch Scott get the shit beat out of him, which was what he imagined Jeff was just about to do...or was he? Did he have something far worse in-store for the guy?

"Are you looking for a good fuck?" Mark heard Jeff snarl at Scott. "Because I think I can help you out."

"No fucking way! You're going to drill me with your cock?" the detained officer shouted. "Well, in the words of your own boy...bring it on fucker!"

"Ok, but it's not my cock you're getting, asshole!"

With Scott easily pinned to the floor, Jeff fiercely began to insert his leather-encased fingers into the man's exposed anus.

Screaming, Scott bellowed as if he were going to be split in two, as each thick digit slid into his prone, moist, shit-chute. Bucking wildly, the officer moaned and groaned, as Jeff relentlessly twisted his meaty hand, swiftly expanding the once tight hole. If Scott could've focused long enough on something besides his ass being ripped open, he would have realized it was a huge mistake on his part to incite such a powerful, aggressive man.

"That's it! Take my fist you fucking pig! Squeal for me!" howled Jeff, plunging deeper. "You thought you were going to bring me down? Use my boy to get to me? Well, look who's fallen now! You're going to be put away for a very long time for what you've done to him! But, guess what? I'm going to walk out of here a new man! Free from all blame thanks to you and your actions. Damn, payback can definitely be a bitch or, in your case, Scott, a fucking pain in the ass!"

Scott thrashed upon the tiled floor with his face twisting into bizarre expressions of both pleasure and pain. One minute he was crying out, begging Jeff to stop, and the next he was moaning as if he were enjoying the assault, becoming accustomed to the invasion.

Mark, trying his hardest to remain focused and detached, found he was becoming oddly aroused by what he was hearing. His cock, fully erect now, was throbbing and pulsating with every moan, groan, and grunt. He could almost feel his seed churning inside his piss slick, plum-size balls.

Jeff, unable at first to see beyond his rage, continued to work on Scott's wet, warm hole, drawing his hand in and out, in and out. Widening the man's chute, his glove became slick in dark, raw juices. As he did this, he too became strangely aroused by the situation, his cock lengthening and trailing along his inner thigh like a snake in heat. If he kept this up, he would most likely cream his uniform pants with a thick, copious load.

Bucking, Scott suddenly squealed, then shouted, "Oh Fuck! Jeff, please...I can't take it...I...can't...take...it! I give in man! Please! Oh...God...stop! You win! You fucking win!"

Looking down, Jeff quickly realized that he had not only successfully worked his fist in, but a good length of his broad forearm. No wonder Scott was crying out for him to stop. Drawing his filth slicked arm out in one long, sweeping motion, Jeff watched, in awe, as Scott's muscular anus swiftly snapped back into shape. However, the river of excrement that flowed from him was enough to force the officer to pull away in disgust, although, not before he fished for the keys to the cuffs holding Mark captive. Grabbing Scott's discarded leather coat, after successfully finding the keys, Jeff proceeded to wipe his dirty arm off all over the satin lining.

"Oh man, sick," Jeff moaned as he got to his booted feet, watching Scott writhe in his own bodily fluids, including gobs of hot jizz, which had erupted from his cock during the assault.

Looking down at his own inflated crotch, Jeff made the wise decision to ignore his pent up, animalistic desires and, instead, quickly moved to get Mark free and out of this hellhole.

"Oh, thank God," cried Mark as Jeff removed his gag.

"Come on, Mark, like I was really going to let him violate you," Jeff firmly replied as he unlocked each set of cuffs.

"Well, I was starting to wonder for a minute," Mark chided as he let his aching arms drop and allowed the ripped up, shredded rags that were once his stunning attire slide off and fall to the floor below.

"Hey, it worked, just like we planned," Jeff whispered as he moved closer to his boy, inspecting him for any marks or scars. "I just knew they had it in for me...and you."

"Yeah, well, next time *you* can be the bait," Mark muttered as he stepped out of his torn pants, leaving him standing in his silk boxers, sheer socks, and leather dress boots, with the stiff, arrow collar and silk bow tie still neatly in place around his neck. "I almost broke down a few times. It was harder than I thought it was going to be."

"Yeah, but, you did great. You've come a long way, Mark, in a really short amount of time. You're no longer that naïve kid I met back at the gym. Nice outfit, by the way. Want to do a few gyrations for me?" Jeff mused to his boy before casually glancing down to Officer Sepe who was...

Gone!

"What the fuck?" Mark cried out, quickly surveying the room for any sign of the man.

"Shit!" Jeff shouted as he bolted for the door. "Stay in here!" he commanded.

Pumping his legs to their full potential, stomping the ground hard in his leather boots, Officer Michaels burst through the outer door of the restroom just in time to see Officer Sepe taking off in Mark's shiny, red sports car.

"Wait! That's my car!" Mark cried out as he came up behind Jeff who was now casually standing in the doorway, watching Scott take off. "You're not going after him?"

"Sorry, Mark," Jeff began with a sympathetic look on his face, "but I was actually hoping he would do that. That tells me he won't be running back to the station anytime soon. He's on the run now. He'll be a wanted man, once we file a few reports."

"Oh," Mark simply replied, but then suddenly questioned, as he noticed only one patrol car in the lot. "What happened to the other guy? Officer Jackson?"

"Funny you should ask," Jeff noted with a wicked grin. "You may not believe this, but...he sold his partner out. Well, at least he thought he did."

"Huh?"

"As soon as Scott brought you up here, to the restrooms, Officer Jackson called me. Little did he know I was right around the corner, already set to swoop in and save your sweet little ass," Jeff concluded with a chuckle and a slap on Mark's firm, silk covered rear.

"Well, oink, oink," cried Mark, dashing off for the warmth of the patrol car. "Oink! Oink!" he jokingly shouted all the way there, with an amazing grin on his gorgeous face.

"Oink, oink," Jeff silently mimicked as he thoughtfully looked to the highway, wondering if or, more importantly, *when* they would see Scott Sepe again. "Oink, oink, indeed, Mark," he repeated, heading to the car, swiftly deciding that he would never let his beautiful, innocent boy be used like this again. Not for a single minute.

THE ABDUCTION OF OFFICER PATRICK CURRAN

Written by: Steve

Officer Patrick Curran fixed the knot of his navy blue tie as he prepared to go on duty. It lay perfectly between the points of the collar of his light blue uniform shirt, just the way he liked it. He pulled on his waist length leather jacket, donned his shiny brimmed cap and took a last look at himself in the mirror before he prepared to make his way to the stables. His knee-high boots shone like mirrors, their spurs gleaming. His dark blue breeches with the yellow stripe running down the sides were spotless. Now he was ready. This was his favorite time of year to patrol

High Park, the autumn air crisp and cool enough for him to wear his jacket, but the brilliant sunshine of the late afternoon made it pleasant to be outside. Perfect weather to arrest miscreants! And there were enough of them around to keep him busy. The fools didn't seem to realize that even the most remote trails in the park were patrolled by mounted policemen. As he swung into the saddle, Patrick felt a tingling in his groin as he recalled his last bust, where he had broken up a drug deal, throwing down to the ground and cuffing one criminal. Too bad the creep's partner had managed to escape. Patrick bet that he wouldn't be hanging around the park in the near future. Oh, how wrong he was!

Nick crouched in the underbrush of the park, waiting patiently. Ever since his friend Paul had been busted, he had been staking out the park, waiting for revenge. The image of the big blond cop knocking Paul to the ground, cuffing him and then rubbing his crotch when he thought that no one could see, was burned into his mind. He was going to get that cop and pay him back, if it was the last thing that he did. He had enlisted his friend Reggie in his scheme, with some misgivings. Reggie hadn't seemed too thrilled with the idea until Nick had described the stocky cop who had arrested Paul. Then Reggie had seemed quite enthusiastic. Nick wasn't quite sure what Reggie had in mind, but at the moment he was settled in the undergrowth a little further down the path, with his slingshot and load of lead pellets. Nick pulled on the cord that he had tied to the lower limbs of the ancient oak on the other side of the trail. It was just the right height to catch the mounted cop across the chest.

Patrick cantered along the paths, which became more and more deserted the further he got from the pond. He had done the usual public relations thing, smiling at the little kids who had waved, excited to see a horse in the park. The families were packing up, getting ready to go as the sun got lower in the sky and the air became cooler. Even the joggers and bike riders started to disappear. The sun still shone brightly, the sky a brilliant blue as he headed deeper into the wilder areas of the park. The light flickered through the brightly colored foliage as he penetrated deeper into the urban wilderness. This was Patrick's favorite time of year, and since the sun was still up, he relaxed in the saddle. He wasn't expecting much trouble at this time of day. It was later, when the sun had set, and most people had left, that the problems started. Then the small time drug dealers emerged, selling their wares mainly to teenagers who lived in the upper middle class areas that surrounded the park. It saved them from going downtown to the seedier areas of the city; and the park gave them the perfect venue to smoke up and drink, away from their parents.

Nick tensed up as he could see the heavyset blond cop approaching. The thinning vegetation and the curves in the path gave him a perfect view of Officer Curran as he made his way along the winding trail. He could see the waning sun shining off the mounted policeman's highly polished leather boots, and gleaming on the shiny brim of his cap. His mouth was dry as he tried to purse up his lips to whistle, the signal that Reggie needed. His first attempt was unsuccessful, but he swallowed a couple of times and was able to fake the call of the cardinal. He hoped that Reggie's aim was as good as he claimed.

Reggie's hands were clammy as he adjusted the slingshot. He was definitely having second thoughts about participating in this scheme. He didn't deal in or use drugs himself, and so far had a clean record. But he had been intrigued by Nick's description of the cop who had arrested their mutual friend Paul. He sounded like just the kind of guy that Reggie would like to have at his mercy, and the fact that he would be in uniform fired his imagination further. He had always found the local mounted cops in their spiffy uniforms extremely sexy, and the thought of having one captive, and wreaking some kind of revenge on him, had clouded his judgment. He just hoped that he could prevent Nick from doing anything too extreme. As he heard the clip clop of the horse's hooves approaching, he pulled up the bandana that he had tied around his neck, covering his face. He took aim just as the mounted policeman passed by, and let go. The lead pellet hit the horse in the rear haunch, just as he had planned. The horse reared on its hind legs, and took off down the path.

As the horse started tearing down the trail, Nick jerked on the cord tied to the tree. It caught the cop across the chest, just as Nick had planned. Officer Curran was jerked out of the saddle and landed with a thud on the soft soil of the path. Nick also covered his face with a bandana, and pulled down his baseball cap to further conceal his face. He ran out of the scrub and towards the police officer, who lay, stunned, on the ground. At the same time, Reggie burst out of the brush, yelling, "It worked, it worked! Just like you said it would!" "Shut up! You want to let everyone in the park know what we're doing? Help me carry the pig into the trees." Nick slid his hands under the armpits of the moaning cop, while Reggie grabbed his booted feet, and the two thugs began carrying the semi-conscious Patrick into the bushes. As they got him off the path, they heard the sound of hooves approaching. "Shit, is there another one coming? There should be only one cop covering this area!" Nick started to panic and dropped Officer Curran's body. Then he relaxed as he realized that it was Curran's rider-less horse returning to the scene. "Reggie, grab the reins of the horse. Lead it into the trees over here, and tie it to one of them. That saves us from having to worry about someone investigating a horse with no cop on it."

Reggie caught the frightened animal, and led it into a deep grove of trees, where he secured it to a thick branch. Then he returned to Nick, who was dragging the cop away from the path. "His hat, where is it?

Shit, it must have fallen off when he got knocked off the horse." "I'll get it," Reggie replied. He darted back onto the trail, and there was the uniform hat, lying in the middle of the trail.

He grabbed it, and as he did so he heard voices, and peering through the trees he saw a couple of joggers approaching. He ran back into the brush where Nick was lying with cop, who was now starting to come back to full consciousness. "People coming – we have to get further into the woods," Reggie hissed. "First, we have to get him blindfolded and cuffed before he comes to." Nick pulled a blue bandana out of his backpack and quickly tied it around Officer Curran's head, tightly knotting it at the back of his head. At the same time Reggie was fumbling with cop's duty belt, getting the handcuffs. The two rolled Curran onto his stomach, and pulling his hands behind his back, secured them with his own handcuffs. The sound of voices became clearer, and at the same time, Patrick regained full consciousness. "What the..." Before he could utter another word Nick turned him over so that the full weight of his body was lying on his cuffed hands. Nick climbed on his chest, clamping his hand over the bound cop's mouth. "Shut the fuck up, pig. You make a noise, you're dead meat." In the meantime, Reggie grabbed the helpless mounted policeman's legs, preventing him from thrashing about and gaining the attention of the passing joggers. Once the couple had passed, Nick released a sigh of relief. "That was too close for comfort. We have to gag him and get him further into the woods, and wait for the sun to set. Then we can move him out of here."

Patrick struggled under the weight of the bodies holding him down. He had a vague recollection of his horse bolting; everything after that was a blur. But now he was fully conscious, aware of the pain in his wrists, the cuffs biting into his flesh, plus that of whoever was sitting on his chest, pushed down on him. He couldn't see anything, feeling cloth tied tightly around his eyes. He tried to cry out for help as he heard voices nearby, but a hand was pressed down over his mouth, keeping him silent. Then he felt something cold and hard pressed against his temple, and a voice threatening him. As the voices faded away the hand was removed from his mouth, but as he opened it to yell, a wadded ball of cloth was shoved into it, deep into his throat. He choked and gagged, but was unable to dislodge it.

Once the danger had passed, Nick removed his hand from Officer Curran's mouth. He already had a balled up bandana at the ready, and as Curran opened his mouth to yell for help, Nick stuffed it in as far as it would go. As he heard the defenseless cop choke on the cloth, he felt a stirring in his groin. He ignored the sensation as he pulled out a pair of grey wool boot socks that he had already tied together at the toes. He placed the big knot formed by the joined socks in between Officer Curran's teeth, and pulled as hard as he could on the ends of the socks. When he saw Curran's cheeks bulging over the resulting tightness, he tied them off at the nape of the neck. Now he wouldn't have to worry about the cop making too much noise. All he could hear were pathetic little mewling noises. "OK, let's get this cop back into the trees. Just in case any one else comes along here. Grab his feet, and I'll take his shoulders."

The two men picked up the bound cop. Patrick squirmed and wriggled, trying to kick out with his booted, bound feet, shrieking obscenities through his gagged mouth. He had no idea who these punks were who had bound, gagged and blindfolded him, but when he got loose, they were going to be sorry. He tugged on the cuffs that bound his hands behind his back, but of course it was useless. There was no way he could get his hands free without the key. He could feel the ropes cutting into his ankles through the leather of his boots, and biting into his knees, just above the tops of his boots. He thrashed about as much he could, intent on giving these two as much trouble as he could.

Nick and Reggie were having a hard time trying to control their captive, even though he was bound and gagged. He wasn't exactly a lightweight, and with him bucking and struggling it was extremely difficult carrying him up the slope of the ravine. The two men were swearing and sweating, even as the air became cooler as the sun fell lower on the horizon. "Drop him here, against this tree" Nick ordered. Reggie was only too glad to comply as he was struck yet again with Officer Curran's booted feet. Once they had dumped the bound officer on the ground, Nick pulled more rope out of his backpack. He tied one end of it around the chain of the handcuffs, and then pulling on the rope hard, and drawing it behind the tree, he attached the other end to the captive's ankles. "Let's see how the bastard likes being hogtied. That might take some of the fight out of him. He can't go anywhere now."

Officer Curran groaned through his gag as his body was painfully arched, the tips of his fingers almost grazing the soles of his boots. He already ached from the fall that he had taken, and within minutes his muscles were protesting against the unnatural position into which they had been forced. The rough wool of the socks that were tied between his teeth chafed the corners of his mouth, and he had to concentrate on not choking on the ball of cloth that filled his mouth. The blindfold was also painfully tight, pressing against his eyes. He tried to yell through the gag, but nothing but incoherent mumbles could be heard.

Nick and Reggie sat on the ground next to their captive, catching their breath. Despite the cool air, they were covered in sweat from lugging the hefty cop up the slope. Nick sniggered as he listened to the pathetic groans of the cuffed cop. "Who's the macho stud cop now? Trussed up like the pig he is, and that nice uniform not quite so spit and polished as it was," he sneered. Reggie kept silent, as his eyes drank in the scene before him. Curran's navy blue tie was hanging out of his jacket, no longer perfectly centered. His breeches were no longer immaculate, but were now covered with bits of leaf and earth. Even the mirror like polish of the boots was scuffed and dimmed. This guy looked so hot! Reggie shifted his position, trying to accommodate his growing erection.

After half an hour, Nick got up. "Time to get moving. We need some light to reach the car. Give me that sack from your backpack." Reggie pulled out the huge canvas mail sack that Nick had given him earlier in the day. Nick undid the rope that attached Officer Curran's hands to his feet. The bound cop grunted in relief as he was released. His relief was short lived; as his two captors shoved him head first into the canvas sack. He panicked as he felt himself being pushed into something that smelled dank and moldy, the little light that had penetrated under the blindfold disappearing. He writhed wildly, but it was too late. Through the canvas he could feel rope being wound around his body. In the stuffiness of the sack he cried out, but no one could hear him.

Once Nick and Reggie had secured their victim inside the sack, they picked it up. Only Officer Curran's booted feet protruded from the mouth of the canvas bag. Now that he was bagged up, it was much easier to carry him. The two men made their way through the deepening gloom along the side of the ravine. The car was parked in a lot that was adjacent to the ravine; all they had to do was to get the cop into the trunk of the car without being detected. By the time they had finally reached the top of the slope, both men were gasping for breath, and bathed in sweat. Even restrained as he was in the sack, the blond cop had kept on struggling. They collapsed on the ground, behind some bushes. Nick crept out to reconnoiter while Reggie lay on top of the bundle that contained Officer Patrick Curran. He could hear the muffled cries for help that came from the gagged cop's mouth. He didn't think that anyone even a few meters away would catch the sound. The cop continued to wriggle and squirm. Reggie had to admire his stamina, but he was looking forward to getting him somewhere secure. Nick came back to where he had left Reggie and Curran. "The coast is clear. There are just a couple of cars left in the lot. And I made to sure to park the car with the trunk facing the ravine. All we have to do is dump him into the trunk, and we're safe." They picked up their burden and lugged it over to the car. Nick had already opened the trunk, and it only took them a moment to drop the captive cop into the trunk, and then slam down the lid.

Patrick moaned in fear as he heard the lid of the trunk close. He could barely breathe, tied up as he was in the sack. A little air must have been making its way in through the opening where his feet were sticking out, but it was incredibly stuffy. He thought that he might suffocate, enclosed in this very confined space, and gagged. He jerked on the cuffs around his wrists, in vain. Even through the canvas he could feel the ropes biting into his body through his uniform. Who were these creeps who had captured him and what were they going to do to him?

Nick drove very carefully, going just above the speed limit, anxious not to draw any attention to himself. It would be awkward to be stopped by a policeman, since he had an officer tied up and gagged in the trunk of the car. Plus, this car didn't belong to him! Old lady Grabowski, who lived on the next street, was visiting her married daughter in Calgary, and he had 'borrowed' her car. He had no intention of letting anything to do with this kidnapping to be connected to him. He had covered the car seat with a blanket, and was wearing gloves. And he was transporting Officer Curran to the Grabowski house. It was located on a very short street, and the house itself was well screened by trees and shrubs, with the back garden bordering the park. It was unlikely that any of the neighbors would notice the car pulling into the driveway, and if they did, they would just think that the old lady had returned earlier than planned. If everything went according to schedule, he would be out of the place in a few hours. He tried to ignore the stiffness in his groin as he approached the house.

Once they reached the house, Nick and Reggie worked quickly. Nick had turned off the headlights as soon as they had turned into the street, and pulling into the driveway, he parked by the back door. They jumped out of the door, opened the trunk and pulled out Officer Curran. Faint moans came from the canvas wrapped bundle as they carried him towards the door. Nick had left it unlocked when he broke into the house the previous night. As soon as they had dropped him on the floor, Nick ran back outside to put the car in the detached garage behind the house. With any luck, no one would have noticed what had just happened.

Left alone in the house, Reggie began undoing the ropes around the sack. His hands trembled as he fumbled with the knots. He was shaking with a mixture of fear and anticipation. He didn't want to get caught, but at the same time he couldn't wait to get his hands on this cop. He wasn't sure what Nick had in mind for their captive; but he knew what he wanted to do. He managed to pull off the heavy canvas, and there laid the prize. The big blond cop was lying moaning on the floor, his hair mussed and uniform somewhat disheveled from his ordeal. He rolled back and forth on the floor, making pitiful choking sounds through the gag. Reggie stayed on his knees, looking at Patrick – at his thick neck above the shirt collar, which was still buttoned, at his cheeks bulging over the tight gag, and as he turned over, at his meaty ass. Reggie reached out and began to unzip Patrick's leather jacket. When he had opened it, he reached inside and began to stroke the cop's stomach. The cop flinched as he felt himself being touched, and cried out through his gag.

Even through the canvas sack, Patrick had felt the cool air when the lid of the trunk was opened. He didn't have enough strength to struggle, half stifled as he was, as he was carried up a couple of steps and dumped on the floor. Then he felt the ropes tied around his body loosen, and the sack was pulled off. He drew in as much air as he could, once he was released from the musty confines of the sack. Patrick moaned as he rolled around on the floor, seeking some relief from his uncomfortable bondage. Then he felt hands touching him, opening his jacket and stroking his stomach. What the hell was going on here! He yelled out through his cloth stuffed mouth.

"Whoa, buddy, hang on a minute. We aren't ready for that, not quite yet." Reggie jumped as Nick entered the kitchen.

His friend had a big grin on his face. "You'll get to play with the cop as much as you want to, but we have some preparations to make first. Help me carry him to the back bedroom. I've got a couple of things set up there. But first, put these on." He tossed Reggie a Spiderman Halloween mask, and a pair of latex gloves. "Why do we need...?" "Just do it. You'll find out in a minute." Nick put on a similar mask and a pair of gloves himself. They picked Patrick up and carried him down the hallway to a small bedroom. "Dump him on the bed, and help me to get his legs and feet untied. Hmm, you'd better sit on his chest; he's starting to bounce around again." Nick said. Their captive was indeed starting to struggle and mmmmpppphhh once more.

Patrick was wondering what kind of nightmare he was in. He had no idea why he had been kidnapped, but he really didn't like what he had heard so far. The words 'play with the cop' terrified him. Was he going to be tortured? He renewed his frantic efforts to get loose, but they were in vain. Even as his feet and legs were freed, he was pinned to the bed as one of his assailants sat on his chest. With his hands cuffed behind his back, there was nothing that he could do but kick out blindly. Then he felt a hand grab one of his feet.

Once the cop's feet and legs were freed, he started thrashing around. It was easy for Nick to dodge the kicking feet, and grab one of them. He had already attached ropes to the corners of the brass bedstead; all he had to do was to loop the rope around one of the booted ankles and tie it off tightly. He repeated the action on the other foot, and then took a step back. He liked what he saw. The big blond cop was lying on the bed with his legs spread wide, tied to the corners of the bed. Nick liked the way that the white rope contrasted with the black leather of the high boots. Reggie was blocking the view of his face, but Nick could hear the cop grunting away through his gag. Nick could feel the nagging pressure in his groin, but he tried to ignore it. He was out for vengeance. Wasn't he? He shook his head, as if to clear it. He had the cop's feet tied the way he wanted, but now it was time for the hands. He had picked this bedroom because of the brass bedstead – the headboard would be perfect for cuffing the cop's hands over his head!

"Help me pull him upright. We have to get at his hands. Here's the key; you unlock the cuffs, while I make sure he doesn't try anything." Nick pulled out the cop's gun and shoved it under his chin. He grabbed Officer Curran's sweat soaked hair and pulled his head back. "You make a move, and I'll blow your head off! You understand? Nod your head." The bound cop had some difficulty in moving his head with Nick's fingers grasping his hair, but he was able to move his head sufficiently to satisfy Nick. In the meantime, Reggie had unlocked the handcuffs. Nick pushed the cop back down on the bed and raised his arms over his head. He threaded the handcuffs through the brass railing and snapped the bracelets shut. He sighed with relief once Officer Curran was firmly secured to the bed. Since he had emptied the bullets from the gun, his threat had been an idle one, and he hadn't looked forward to having to bash the guy over the head with the gun. That would have interfered with his plans.

Nick slid off the bed and motioned Reggie to follow him out into the hall. As they left the room, they could hear Officer Curran yelling through his gag, and the rattle of the handcuffs chain on the brass headboard as he tugged on his bound hands. The whole bed was creaking as he struggled, him trying to free his feet from the ropes that bound them to the foot of the bed, but both the bonds and the bed held firm. "I've got a digital camera and a camcorder in there. This is what we're going to do." Nick leaned over and whispered his plans into Reggie's ear. Reggie's mouth went dry and his knees felt weak as Nick told him what he wanted to do. This was a dream come true! His cock became hard as a rock as Nick outlined his plan for vengeance on the hefty blond cop who was lying bound, gagged and blindfolded in the bedroom. He couldn't wait to start.

Patrick pulled and pulled on the handcuffs, hoping against hope that somehow he could get his hands free, but it was futile. He moved his head back and forth against the pillows upon which it was resting, and to his joy, he realized that the gag was coming loose! He worked his jaw back and forth, and rubbed his head against the pillow even harder. The rough woolen socks that held the balled up bandana inside his mouth finally slipped down around his neck. He pushed with his tongue and the cloth came out of his mouth. The inside of his mouth was parched; the bandana that had been stuffed into it had absorbed all of his saliva. He worked his tongue around his mouth and sucked in some air. The relief at getting the gag out of his mouth was immense. Then he tried to yell.

As Nick and Reggie re-entered the room, they immediately saw the grey boot socks had fallen down around Officer Curran's neck, and the sodden bandana was resting on top of them. Just as he opened his mouth to cry out for help, Nick uttered a stifled curse and dove for the bed. He landed on the cuffed cop before he could utter a word. All the air in the cop's lungs was driven from his body as Nick's body slammed into his. As he struggled to breathe, Nick slapped his hand over his mouth. "Hey, buddy, get my backpack from the kitchen. I've got just the thing in it so this little piggy can't try to huff and puff and blow the house down." When Reggie returned with the backpack, he was already rummaging inside it. "This what you wanted?" he said, as he pulled out a roll of black duct tape. "That's it. Pull off a nice long piece for me." As he could hear Reggie ripping off a piece of the tape, Nick picked up the soaked bandana that Curran had spat out just moments before. He removed his hand from the cop's lips and held the ball of cloth against them. "Open wide, big boy. I've something here for you to chew on."

Patrick groaned with frustration as he felt the wet cloth being jammed against his lips. He kept his teeth clenched and his lips pressed together. Now that he had managed to get some breath into his lungs he tried to raise his torso from the bed as high as he could, in an effort to dislodge the man sitting on his chest. He wasn't successful, but he wrenched his head to one side, trying to prevent the bandana from being stuffed back into his mouth. Even as he struggled, he became aware that his cock was stiffening. Great, he thought. Here I am cuffed and blindfolded and about to be gagged, and I'm getting an erection. He redoubled his efforts to evade the cloth that Nick was attempting to insert into his mouth.

"Boy, we've got a live one here, don't we? Pinch his nostrils shut for me." Nick grabbed what he could of Curran's short blond hair, pulling his head back, all the time keeping the wadded bandana pressed against the cop's mouth. When Reggie leaned over and held the cop's nose between his fingers, Curran was eventually forced to open his mouth to breathe. As soon as he did, Nick shoved the cloth into his mouth, pushing his fingers inside to make sure that it went in far enough. Reggie then plastered the piece of tape over the cop's mouth, sealing in the bandana. Reggie winced as he heard Officer Curran choke on the gag. He didn't want to hurt this guy. He would have to be careful with Nick, and make sure that he didn't go too far.

Nick got off the bed, wiping his flushed face. He could no longer ignore the fact that he had a raging erection. One of the reasons that he had brought Reggie in on this was because he had been fairly certain, from remarks that he had made, that he would enjoy humiliating a bound and gagged cop. What Nick hadn't counted on was his own reaction. As he looked down on the trussed and gagged officer, his mind was whirling. His desire for revenge was now mixed with the desire for something else. He shook himself, and turned to his accomplice. "Get to it. You know what you have to do."

Reggie sat down on the side of the bed and ran trembling hands over the captive cop's chest. He heard the cop grunt through the gag as he felt the unseen hands start to stroke his torso. "Wait, prop him up on the pillows, and put this on him." The cop's shiny brimmed cap came flying through the air and landed on the bed. Reggie placed it on Officer Curran's head, and then pushed the pillows from the bed under his shoulders. He began stroking the cop again, pushing the navy blue tie to one side as he rubbed his chest. Even through the cop's shirt and undershirt, he could feel his captive's nipples harden. Before he could do more, Nick called out to him again. "Stop, and take off his blindfold. I want good clear shots of his face. And I want him to see what is happening. That's why we have these stupid masks on, so he can't identify us." Reggie reached behind Curran's head, and started fumbling with the knots in the blue bandana that blindfolded the cop. Nick had tied it so tight Reggie had some difficulty, but finally he had it untied, and threw it to one side. The policeman blinked at the light, moaning with relief as the blindfold was removed.

Patrick blinked as the light hit his eyes. He had been tightly blindfolded for hours, so the removal of the piece of cloth that had been tied around his head was a great relief. It took a few moments for his eyes to readjust, and then he looked around him. He saw two men wearing Halloween masks, one sitting on the bed next to him, the other standing across the room. The second man was holding a camera, and even as Patrick looked at him, he took a picture. What the Hell was going on here? Then the guy who was sitting on the bed next to Patrick starting rubbing his chest again. Patrick moaned as he felt his nipples harden, and was acutely conscious of the growing bulge in his breeches. With his legs spread wide open, he feared that it must be obvious to at least one of the men that he had an erection.

"Ha, the cop's got a woody! This makes it even better! Work him over, buddy." Nick chortled. Reggie barely heard him as he started to unbutton the cop's uniform shirt. He undid the tie as he opened the top button, letting his fingers linger on the thick neck. Then he slowly undid the rest of the buttons, listening

71

to the cop whimper as his shirt was pulled open and his white undershirt pushed up his chest. As Reggie leaned over to lick the protuberant nipples he let one hand slide down the cop's belly until it had reached his groin. He kneaded the lump that he found there, feeling it grow under his hand. He unzipped the uniform trousers and slid his hand inside until he found the fly of the boxers. Yep, there was something hard and growing inside; Nick would be pleased. That was what he wanted – pictures of this big blond cop tied up and gagged, being worked over by another guy and sporting a hard on. Reggie had to dig around a bit before he was able to extract the swollen member from the underwear. He heard the cop making louder moans and looked up at the captive's face. Officer Curran was shaking his head from side to side, and even through the gag Reggie could hear a muffled "No, No." He could see the cop's grey eyes pleading with him. Reggie just smiled under his mask and started licking the big guy's nipples. He let the fingers of one hand lightly caress the cop's hard cock, while he used the fingers of his other hand to run up down Curran's rib cage. He used just the tips of his fingertips, letting them graze the flesh. He wasn't sure which of his actions was producing the loudest grunts: his lips and tongue on the sensitive nipples, his hand on the cock or his fingers tickling the ribs. Perhaps he should experiment.

Nick was clicking away with the camera, and adjusting the camcorder as needed. He couldn't wait to show the cop the pictures of him all tied up with a hard cock. This was just the beginning! It looked like Reggie was just getting started. It should get much better. Nick shifted position, adjusting his underwear. He wasn't supposed to be reacting like this! He had thought that Reggie might be able to get the cop hard, but...Nick didn't think that he would be sporting an erection himself. But...listening to the guy in uniform grunting through his gag, struggling in his bondage on the bed...Nick was getting horny.

Reggie pulled off the gloves. He wanted to feel the flesh

of the bound cop against his fingertips. He tossed them to one side and renewed his attack on Curran's body. He took one the cop's nipples between his teeth and nibbled on it, while slightly increasing the intensity of his strokes on the cock. He heard the rattle of the handcuffs on the brass headboard as his captive pulled on his cuffed hands, groaning through his tape-gagged mouth. He was shaking his head from side to side, his cap sliding down over his brows as he struggled. 'MMMNOOOOPHHH".

Patrick tugged desperately on his cuffed hands as he felt his nipple being taken between his tormentor's teeth. NO! His nips were so sensitive...the gentle pressure was driving him crazy. And that hand on his cock...He couldn't help himself as he started to arch his hips, trying to increase the friction. His mind was in a whirl as his body betrayed him. He had always got a thrill out of cuffing perps, but...to be cuffed and gagged while wearing his uniform, and having some guy molesting him, and to be hard as a rock and desperate to cum...This couldn't be happening to him! He tried to get his feet loose, yanking on the ropes that bound them as hard as he could, but the only result was that he could feel the rope cutting through the leather of his boots, biting into his ankles. The sight of the white rope disappearing into his boots made him even hornier. If only the guy jerking him off would do it a little bit harder...Sweat drenched his body, soaking into his uniform.

Reggie moved his mouth down his captive's body. He stuck his tongue into Curran's navel, licking the sweat that had accumulated there, twirling his tongue around the navel, being rewarded by more frantic groans. Then he slowly began unbuckling the cop's belt, while continuing to jerk on his hard cock. He wanted to get those breeches down, so he could see the whole picture, as it were. Once he had the belts unbuckled, he undid the breeches and pulled them down, along with the cop's underwear. Now his genitals and thighs were fully exposed. As he continued to pump, slower and then faster, he began licking the tender flesh of Curran's inner thighs. He could feel the muscles flex as the bound cop jerked on the ropes that tied his feet to the corners of the bed. Reggie let his tongue flicker upwards, just brushing the cop's balls. He heard a gagged yowl as he did this, and decided to engulf the whole sac with his mouth.

Nick had been darting around the bed, snapping pictures, putting down the camera and grabbing the camcorder as Reggie moved around on the bed. This was going to be great! When they were finished the cop would have to resign from the force. This guy was obviously getting off on what was being done to him; he had been sporting an erection even before Reggie had touched his cock. Or...maybe Nick could get him to refuse to testify when Paul went to trial. He could lose the paperwork or something like that. Nick was a bit hazy about the working of the legal system, but he was sure that something could be arranged. There was no way that this seemingly straight cop would want the pictures that Nick was taking to be sent to his co-workers, or enlarged and plastered to the walls of the police station. And the video that he was recording should prove to be interesting viewing. Nick rubbed his crotch as he paused. This scene was really turning him on.

Patrick was bouncing up and down on the bed, as much as his bonds permitted. He dug his fingernails into the palms of his hands as Reggie started sucking on his balls. Oh, that felt so good. And then...Reggie stopped. He removed his hand and his mouth from Patrick's genitals, and sat back on his haunches. "How does that feel, big boy? You want me to stop? Or should I continue? Hmmm?" Reggie taunted him. Patrick was torn. Did he really want this to continue? And would his captors pay any attention to him, even if he shook his head in the negative? He didn't think so. But...he had to try – even though he thought that his balls would explode if he didn't cum soon. "MMSTOPMMPPH," was the sound the captive cop made.

"You sure that's what you want?" Reggie asked and picked up the discarded bandana that had been used a blindfold and brushed it against the tip of Patrick's cock. Patrick grunted through his gag as he felt the material sliding back and forth, teasing him. He raised his hips trying to get more. Reggie laughed. "Buddy, you getting this all on tape? I think the cop is saying that he doesn't want any more, but his cock seems to be singing a different tune. How about this, big guy? You want me not to do this to you?" Reggie leaned over and started blowing on Patrick's cock, his mouth just an inch away. Patrick twisted and struggled, trying to evade that hot breath that felt so good, and the caressing of his cock head with the bandana, which was driving him crazy. No, he didn't want this. He REALLY didn't want this! Damn, this guy, why wouldn't he jerk him off? "MMMMPPHHHHHHH!"

As Reggie teased and tormented the captive cop, he finally allowed one of his hands to move to his own crotch. He massaged his swollen cock through his khakis while he continued to blow on Officer Curran's erection. He was so turned on he wished that this could last for days. Having this big beefy cop trussed up and gagged was making him so horny he could barely control himself. He dropped the bandana and slid his free hand under the cop's meaty ass. Ummm, that felt good. He caressed the buttock while he sent gusts of hot air towards the erection that was bobbing just in front of his eyes. Listening to the cop groaning through the gag was such a turn on for him. The more noise that he made, muffled as it was by the bandana stuffed into his mouth and the tape that sealed it in, the hornier Reggie became. That mmmmpppphing was so sexy. He let his mouth get a little closer to the cop's dick, and flicked his tongue out. He let just the tip of it touch the shaft. As he became more engrossed in what he was doing, he was barely conscious of Nick moving around in the background.

Nick was becoming more and more agitated as he filmed the scene that was unfolding before his eyes. This was supposed to be about revenge and humiliation! It had started off well, but now he could hear Reggie making little noises in his throat – he seemed to be slowing down and getting gentler with every passing moment. And the cop was enjoying this far too much. Nick had wanted incriminating photos and videotape, which he now had, but it all seemed too easy. Curran wasn't even fighting as much against his molestation as he had at first. For blackmail purposes that was great; it would show that this guy was just a big perv, but still...something was missing. It seemed as if Reggie was concentrating on giving the cop pleasure. That wasn't what Nick had had in mind. He bit his lip, trying to dismiss the raging hard-on in his jeans. But he couldn't. He had to change the dynamics of this situation – he had to show who was really in charge.

Reggie opened his own zipper and slid his hand inside his khakis. He pulled himself up and let his mouth move a little further up. He took the head of Curran's cock in his mouth, letting his tongue play with it. The cop pushed his hips up, trying to shove more of his cock down Reggie's throat. Reggie pulled back and chuckled. "Not so fast, big guy, you're not going to get that yet." Reggie moved his mouth up Officer Curran's belly, leaving a wet trail of saliva as he made his way to the cop's erect nipples. He pulled his hand out of his own crotch, and started stroking on Curran's instead. Very lightly, very gently, but it was enough to get a reaction. He felt the cop's big body jerk. Reggie pulled off the nipples and looked into Curran's face. His eyes were pleading with Reggie, and he could hear him whimpering beneath the gag. His uniform hat had fallen off in the course of his struggles and now lay on the pillow next to his head. The knotted grey work socks were still hanging around his thick neck, resting on his pushed up tee shirt. The cop looked so vulnerable lying there, with his hands cuffed over his head, and his mouth taped shut, that Reggie nearly shot his own load. Soon, very soon...maybe he could get seconds, or even thirds! It depended on how much time Nick gave him.

Patrick squirmed desperately in his bonds. He had been so

close – if the guy in the mask had just kept his mouth on his cock for a minute longer, he would have cum. He yanked futilely at his cuffed hands, rattling the chain, but nothing gave. Through the mask he made eye contact with his tormentor. The guy started moving his mouth back down Patrick's body, over his belly, down further...Oh God, oh yes...He was taking Patrick's cock in his mouth again, but this time he was taking more in ...not just the head...that hot mouth was engulfing all of him, swallowing him down whole...the tongue working his head...oh God...Patrick reared up as much as he could, shoving his cock down as far as possible...no withdrawal this time...no retreat...the cuffs were biting into his wrists, the ropes into his ankles through his boots, but he didn't care...UNH UNNHHHHHHH!

Reggie pulled his head back as the cop started to spurt. Semen flew in a spray like a fountain, shooting all over the cop's belly and chest. Reggie worked the erupting cock with his hand, urging out yet more cum, polishing the red head of the cock with his thumb. Spasm after spasm shook the hefty cop's body. Reggie could hear him squealing behind his gag as he struggled against the ropes and cuffs as he exploded. Finally, Reggie let go of the cop's cock. His victim lay back, his eyes closed, sobbing through his gag, his upper body covered in his own thick and gooey cum. Some had even splattered on his opened uniform shirt. Reggie could see the sweat running down Curran's face, and down his body. Reggie was just reaching back inside his khakis for his own cock, when he felt a hand on his shoulder.

Nick had had enough of standing around and filming the scene. He had recruited Reggie because he thought that Reggie would be able to get the cop sexually excited, and he had. But now Nick found himself in a surprising state of sexual arousal, and he wanted to get off. Reggie was being way too nice to the cop – Nick had heard him murmuring to his captive, in a gentle tone. This didn't fit into his plans. He wanted revenge and humiliation – and now Reggie was going all soft and tender on him. Nick was just waiting for him to start kissing the cop, or something stupid like that. He was going to show these two who was the boss! Once he had videotaped Curran shooting his load, he strode over to the bed and grabbed Reggie by the shoulder. "OK, my turn. You hold the camera while I have some fun with the pig." "But you said that you didn't..." "Yeah, yeah, well I've changed my mind. Get out of the way. I'm going to change the cop's gag for him. Let's see how he likes chewing on a beef gag!"

Nick pulled Reggie off the bed, and thrust the camcorder into his hands. Then he hopped onto the bed and straddled the helpless cop, sitting on his chest. Nick undid his heavy leather belt and then his jeans. He pushed them down, and then pulled down his boxers. His erect cock was waving in the air, just inches away from the cuffed cop's face. He saw Curran's eyes bulge in horror. The cop tried to squirm away from him, but tied as he was no escape was possible. Nick rubbed his cock over Curran's face, laughing as the cop pressed his head down into the pillows, trying to evade the hard cock. "Yeah, got ready to choke, big man. Let's see the macho cop eat dick!" His captives muffled cries of horror coming from beneath the gag made Nick even hornier. As he ripped the strip of duct tape from Curran's face, his mind was racing. He hadn't thought that he would want to do this, but seeing the cop all tied and gagged, and what Reggie had done to him, had inflamed him beyond belief. He stuck his fingers into Curran's mouth and extracted the sopping wet bandana, reduced by now to a compact ball. "Please, no, don't do..." Before Patrick could get another word out, Nick plunged in. He grabbed the ends of the cop's tie, which was lying undone around his neck, and pulled on it, wrapping the cloth around his fists. This had the effect of raising Curran's head up higher, holding it close to Nick's crotch. Nick started rocking back and forth, pumping in and out, in and out, ignoring the retching sounds coming from the cop's plugged throat.

Reggie stood in a corner of the room, aghast at the turn

of events. Nick had roped him into this affair because he knew that Reggie was gay, and had a taste for bondage AND cops. But Nick...Nick was straight! He had a volatile temper, which was why Reggie thought that he might have to intervene at some point, but the manic gleam in his eyes had warned Reggie off. There was no knowing what Nick might do if Reggie tried to stop him now. It could be something far worse than what was happening at the moment. The look on Nick's face as he shoved himself back and forth into the helpless cop's mouth scared Reggie. He winced in sympathy as he heard the gurgled cries coming from Officer Curran's throat. Then he noticed that the cuffed officer's cock was no longer flaccid. It had to come to life again, and was sticking up straight into the air. Hmm, this was an interesting development.

Patrick had watched in horror as the first masked guy who had brought him off was shoved aside by the man who had been filming the scene. He had grunted in dismay as this guy dropped his jeans and boxers and thrust his cock into Patrick's face. Patrick had felt the stickiness of the pre-seminal fluid on his cheeks and had tugged futilely at his bonds as he realized what was about to happen to him. When the tape had been brutally ripped from his face, and the soppy bandana pulled out of his mouth, he had tried to plead for mercy, but his words had been cut off abruptly as the hard cock was shoved deep into his throat. He had never had another guys cock in his mouth before this. He gagged as the cock plunged into his throat and tried to fight it off, but it was no use. It was impossible for him to try to get his head away as his own necktie was used to hold his head in place, mashing his face against the crotch of his captor. He sniffed in the musky smell. And then sniffed some more. Hmmm. The pressure on his neck and shoulders was almost intolerable, the big dick plunging back and forth in his throat was almost choking him, but...he felt his own cock start to harden again. What was going on here? Why was his body reacting this way?

Nick gritted his teeth and grunted as he moved his hips

back and forth. He hoped that Reggie was catching this on tape. This would teach the cop to be careful whom he messed with. Nick kept on telling himself that was the only reason he was doing this – revenge. Sweat was pouring down his face, veins bulging. Oh boy...this felt good. Not bad for a first timer, if this was the cop's first time! He dropped the ends of the necktie and instead clamped his hands on the back of Curran's head, holding it tight, jamming it into his crotch. He could hear the cop making noises, mmmphing away. Oh yeah...this was good. Nick bit down on his lip. He couldn't last...not fair...but watching Reggie work the cop over had been too much for him...he couldn't hold on any longer...shit, this guy had a hot tight mouth...

Officer Rodney Graham was nearing the end of his shift. He had promised his aunt Sophie to check out her house every night. He turned into her quiet street and pulled into the driveway. He got out of the car and started checking the doors and windows. When he reached the kitchen door at the side, he noticed two things simultaneously. The door was ajar, and he could see a thin thread of light shining into the garden from one of the back windows. He was certain that none of the lights back there were on a timer, and the open door made him very suspicious. He pulled his gun from its holster, and quietly made his way into the house. As he moved down the back hall, he could see that the door to the spare bedroom was open, and light was flooding through it. He could hear moans and groans coming from the room. What the hell was going on here? He paused on the threshold, and a shocking sight met his eyes. He could see booted legs tied to the corners of the bed, with uniform breeches pushed down to the knees. The face of the tied man was obscured by another man sitting on his chest, rocking back and forth. As Rodney watched, he heard one of the men utter a guttural yell. "Fuck, I'm cumming in this cop's mouth. Unnnhhhhhh!" Rodney darted through the door. "Hands up!"

Reggie had heard steps approaching. He had retreated

into a corner of the room, behind the door. He was panic stricken, and did not know what to do. He heard a sudden intake of breath from the hallway, and then the words "Hands up!" Instinctively, Reggie shoved the door forward with all his might, and felt it slam into a body. He heard a groan and then the thump of someone falling to the floor. He moved from behind the door and saw another police officer lying prone, moaning. His hands were shaking in fear as Nick pulled out of the helpless Officer Curran's mouth. "Oh fuck, what's this. Another one! Here, get him cuffed while I gag this one." Nick grabbed the wet ball of bandana, and shoved it back into Officer Curran's mouth. He pulled up the knotted work socks, and tightened them, fixing the bandana in place. Officer Curran looked miserable as he was bandanna and sock gagged again. Then Nick turned his attention to the new arrival.

Reggie was gingerly pulling the fallen cop's handcuffs from his duty belt. He knelt there, and started to attach one of the bracelets to a wrist. Nick pushed him out of the way. "Look in my knapsack; I think that there is something in there to stuff his mouth with. And get the tape. Hurry, before he comes completely to!" Reggie delved into Nick's knapsack, but all that he could find to use as a gag was a pair of athletic socks. He picked up the roll of duct tape, and with the socks and tape in hand, he made his way over to Nick, who having cuffed the cop's hands behind his back, was now pulling off his necktie, and wrapping it around his captive's eyes as a blindfold. The cop was moaning as his tie was bound tightly around his head. Nick turned around and saw Reggie. "Quick, give me one of those socks, and tear off a piece of the tape" Nick balled up the white sock, and grabbing the cop by his light brown hair, he yanked his head up, and stuffed the sock into his open mouth. The cop had had no idea what was coming, and was unable to offer any resistance. As he choked on the sock that was shoved into his mouth, Nick slapped the strip of tape over his lips, sealing it in. "There you go, buddy, now I've given you something else to play with. Go to it!"

Reggie looked down at the cop who was lying bound, gagged and blindfolded on the floor. This was one was even cuter than the first! He looked to be about 33, 5'9" tall, with light brown hair. While not as stocky as Officer Curran, he looked damn hot. Reggie's cock became hard again. He had not been able to satisfy his desire earlier, since Nick had pushed him out of the way. He licked his lips. This time he was going to get his way. The cop looked so vulnerable laying there, his light blue shirt pulled open at the collar, exposing his white crew tee shirt. His navy jacket was half off his shoulders and his shiny brimmed peaked cap was lying on the floor next to him. Reggie couldn't wait to get to work on - he peered at the cop's badge- Officer Rodney Graham.

Patrick looked with horror at the scene that was unfolding in front of him. He had had his face still crushed into his captor's groin, struggling not to choke on the jism that was flooding his throat, when he heard the fracas in the doorway. When he heard the words "Hands up" he thought that he was saved, but those words were followed far too soon by the sound of a thud, and then something heavy falling to the floor. Nick pulled out of his mouth, but before Patrick had a chance to call out for help, or even to spit out the cum in his mouth, the loathsome spitty bandana was pushed back into his mouth, and tied into place. And then those damned thick work socks used to keep the bandanna in place. Once Nick had jumped off the bed, Patrick had a view of what was going on. He could see his two masked captors binding and gagging another policeman who was lying on the floor. As he watched the new captive's head being pulled and a white sock stuffed into his mouth, Patrick felt and saw his own cock getting even harder, especially when he heard the grunt that came from the stuffed mouth.

Rodney lay on the floor in a daze, as his hands were dragged behind him and secured with his own handcuffs. He could do nothing as he felt his uniform tie being yanked off and tied around his eyes. As his head was pulled up by the hair, he opened his mouth to protest. As he did so, a ball of cloth was pushed into his mouth. Before he was able to spit out, he felt something sticky plastered across his lips. He realized that there were at least two men tying him up, but blindfolded as he was with his necktie, he could see nothing, just a little light penetrating beneath the blindfold. He thought back to what he had seen just before he had been overpowered. A guy in what looked to be a mounted police officer's uniform, tied to the bed and apparently being sexually molested. Was this going to happen to him? No way, not if he could help it!

Nick picked up one of the discarded lengths of rope that had been used to bind Officer Curran before he was tied to the bed. He grabbed one of the cop's ankles, preparing to tie his feet together. To his surprise the cop kicked out at him and, heaving his body up from the floor, attempted to get to his knees. The blow had caught Nick in the chest, knocking him to the floor. Reggie stood stunned as their latest victim staggered to his feet. The cuffed cop, disoriented by the blindfold, started lumbering across the room. Reggie wrapped his arms around him, trying to hold him still, but the cop struggled vigorously in his grasp, kicking out and twisting, trying to get free of the arms that held him. The two struggling men's feet became entwined, and they both fell to the floor, with the cop on the bottom. While Reggie tried to restrain the struggling cop, he could feel the bound body writhing beneath, and hear Rodney grunting and cursing through his stuffed and taped mouth. With his own body pressed into the cop's, Reggie could feel his cock stiffen as it rubbed against his writhing captive. The fall had further weakened Officer Graham, and Reggie had his chin pressed down on the back of his head, holding him against the floor. He could see the knot of the necktie blindfold, pressing into the light brown hair. Oh God, this was turning him on. His momentary panic had disappeared, and now he was horny. He couldn't wait to get started on this one.

"OK, smart ass cop – you're going to wish that you hadn't

done that." Nick got to his feet, rubbing his chest where the cop's foot had struck him. He picked up the rope and stretched it between his hands, pulling on it. "Keep him pinned down, buddy. This little piggy is going to get his feet tied really good and tight. He won't be going anywhere for a while." Nick once again got a grasp on one of the struggling cop's feet, this time making sure that he didn't get kicked. He knotted one end of the rope around the ankle and then began wrapping the rope around both ankles, before tying it off. He pulled on the rope as hard as he could, and was rewarded when he heard a muffled grunt from Rodney as the rope bit into his ankles. He gave the cop a slap on the ass before he got to his feet. "Go ahead, buddy, have some fun with this cop. Two on film is even better than one."

Reggie got off the cop, and rolled him over on to his back. He heard the cop moan as the full weight of his body landed on his cuffed hands. Reggie unbuttoned the shirt and pulled the white tee shirt over the cop's head, exposing his bare chest. He ran his hands over the chest, tweaking the nipples. "MMMMFFUMCKMPASSHLMPH." Officer Graham's body jerked on the floor as he swore beneath his gag. He kicked out with bound feet and tried to roll away from the probing hands. Reggie pushed down on his shoulders and then straddled his thighs, pinning him to the floor, before he began working on his captive's torso. He rubbed the nipples between thumb and forefinger, slid his hands under the opened shirt, running his fingers down the rib cage. He started to knead the cop's stomach, slowly moving his hands further down his body towards the belt buckle. And all the time Rodney fought against him, bound and gagged though he was.

Rodney bucked in his bondage, attempting to throw off the man who was straddling him. He yelled through his gag, trying not to flinch as he felt hands moving over his body. He didn't want to reveal how sensitive he was; for fear that these two would do even worse things to him. Even as he thought this, he could feel his nipples harden. And once again the picture of the guy tied to the bed came to mind. One thing that he had tried to block out was the fact that the man tied to the bed, apparently being forced to give head, had been sporting an enormous erection. Were these two going to do the same thing to him? Was he going to be sexually molested? At that moment he felt the hands move further down his body, and start to caress his groin. Shit!

Reggie was enjoying the feistiness of his new victim. The struggling and mmmphhing just made him more intent on teasing the bound cop. He let his hands stray below the belt, to the navy blue clad crotch. Hmm. This one wasn't hard like the mounted cop had been – at least he wasn't hard yet. Reggie would have to see what he could do about that! He started massaging the cop's groin, very gently, at first. It didn't take too long for something hard to start forming inside the uniform pants. Reggie increased the pressure, and moved one hand back up to the cop's torso. He slowly let his hand move up to the erect nipples, poking a finger into the navel on his way up. This guy was really trying to fight him, but to no avail. The cop couldn't hide the effect that Reggie's caresses were having on him, no matter how hard he tried. His face was turning red, at least the parts that weren't obscured by the tape and the necktie. Reggie almost lost his balance as Officer Rodney tried to raise himself from the floor, but he kept on working away. He stopped for a moment, as he pulled down the zipper of the uniform pants and slid his hand inside. The cop went crazy then, screaming through his gag in protest, trying to roll from side to side in an effort to escape the invading hand, but it was useless. Reggie found the fly of the briefs, and inserted his fingers.

Propped on the pillows on the bed, Patrick watched with dread fascination as his fellow police officer was abused. He jerked on his bonds, with no real hope of getting free. His cock was hard as a rock, as he listened to the gagged moans of the man on the floor. He lifted his head in an attempt to get a better view. Was his fellow victim going to be treated the same that Patrick had been? If so, he wanted to watch. Mmmm, he could use a hand right now, strategically placed, or even better...Patrick was shocked at his own thoughts. He should be concentrating on getting free. But...he knew that he couldn't escape from the cuffs, and if someone decided to molest him again, and force him to cum, there wasn't anything that he could do to stop it. He was helpless. Totally helpless.

In the meantime Rodney renewed his struggles to escape. He could feel a hand moving inside his briefs, finding the penis that had hardened as a result of the massaging. He couldn't help his reaction; it could happen to anyone! He pulled at the cuffs securing his aching wrists, but they held firm. He tried rubbing his head against the floor in an attempt to get rid of the blindfold – if he was able to see he might have more luck in fighting against the man who was molesting him. OH SHIT! He felt the hand grasp his cock and pull it out of his briefs. The hand disappeared, but then he felt something warm blowing against it. What was going on? Whatever it was, it felt good. Rodney's cock stirred, growing harder. NO! He wasn't going to let this happen. He wrenched his body to one side in an effort to evade the hot breath, but he was pinned down again. He heard a low chuckle. "You're not going anywhere, Officer Graham, not for a while. We're going to have a little fun." The hand was on Rodney's cock again, stroking it gently but firmly. Rodney tried to push out the sock that had been stuffed into his mouth, but the tape wouldn't budge. He moaned in humiliation as he became more and more physically excited. Then he felt his belt being unbuckled, and his trousers were undone. He tried to push his buttocks down against the floor as his uniform trousers and his briefs were pulled down, after his hard cock was disentangled from the briefs. "MMMNOMMPHH!"

Reggie's cock was rock hard inside his khakis. He didn't know how long he could hold out, since Nick had interrupted him the first time, before he could cum. He didn't want to hurry this scene – this guy was so appealing, lying there in front of him, bound and gagged. Just enough meat on his bones to make him interesting. The way that he had fought against Reggie made it more fun. What else could he do? Reggie slid a bit further down the cop's legs, and while he kept on stroking the cop's cock, he started brushing the inside of the cop's thighs with his fingers. Bingo! Officer Graham screamed through his gag once more, and renewed his thrashing, but it was to no avail. Reggie kept a firm grip on the cock while he moved his fingers back and forth, just touching the skin, letting them flick against the cop's balls before he moved back down. After doing that for a few minutes, he removed his hand from the thighs, and used it to support himself as he leaned over. Time for some tongue work now! He used his tongue to retrace the path that his fingers had taken, licking the inside of the thighs, flicking the balls with the tip of his tongue, all the time continuing jerking off the cop, slowly but surely. He was getting whimpering sounds now, so he slowed down even more. He didn't want this guy to spurt too soon! He ran his tongue over the head of the cock – desperate whimpers now. "MMMMMPHHHNOHHUNNO." The sound was music to Reggie's ear. He shifted position as he tongue probed the navel, swirling around and around. Then, very slowly, he moved further up the cop's body, licking his stomach until he reached the erect nipples. The cop was moving his body up and down now as much as he could, trying to hump Reggie's hand. Once Reggie had one of the nipples in his mouth, holding the nub very gently between the edges of his teeth while he manipulated with his tongue, the cop went crazy. Arching his body up and crying out through his sock stuffed and taped mouth. Reggie could see that the cop's hair was wet, soaked with sweat as he struggled. He had to be careful or this guy was going to blow his load before Reggie was ready for him.

Nick had picked up the camcorder and had been taping the scene. Reggie was a true artist! It had taken some time, but he had the second cop hard and moaning, just as he had done with Curran. Having a second cop bound and helpless and hard was an added bonus. Nick had an idea – something that would complete Officer Curran's humiliation. He turned the camcorder towards the cop bound to the bed, noting with satisfaction that he was still sporting a woody, and was watching the scene in front of him with avid attention. Hmm, yes, this would work.

Rodney couldn't believe what was happening to him. This bastard was finding his weak points, one after another. Here he was, tied up and gagged while wearing his uniform, and he was desperate to cum because another guy was working him over! He moaned with pleasure and despair as he felt his nipple being sucked, half wishing that the man who was tormenting him would jerk on his cock harder. He wanted to shoot. And then the mouth left his nipple and started to move higher up his body. Oh no. He started to squirm as felt the tongue in the hollow of his neck and then...AAGGGGHHHH. The tongue was under the blindfold, in his ear. He jerked his head away, and then there was hot breath blowing in his ear, on the nape of his neck. And still, the hand working away on his cock, faster and then slower. He began thrashing about, trying to ignore the pain in his cuffed wrists, pinned beneath his body. Oh God, this was torture. Oh, why didn't he suck the end of his cock again? Rodney could feel the sweat running down his body as he struggled. Then the bastard started licking the sweat running down the back of his neck. 'MMMMMPPHHHH."

Reggie lapped up the sweat trickling down the back of his captive's neck. Umm yeah, it was having the requisite effect. That always got them. The skin there was so soft and smooth and sensitive. Nothing like a little gentle torture to get a guy going. And he was going himself! The pressure in his groin was almost unbearable. This evening was turning out hotter than he had ever expected. If he could just last a few more minutes... Reggie was drenched in sweat himself. He wished that he could remove his mask, which was becoming seriously uncomfortable, but with the cop on the bed without a blindfold, he couldn't risk removing the mask. He started moving south again, all the time gently pumping on the cuffed cop's hard cock. The sound of the muffled whimpers was really turning him on. He worked his way down the cop's torso, running his tongue over every inch of available skin. He had to get his hand inside his own trousers soon, this was driving him crazy. Reggie probed the navel of the cop with his tongue on his way down; almost there! Once he got the cop off he could let himself go! Ah, there was the hard cop cock, almost poking him in the eye. Once he got his mouth around that, Reggie didn't think that he would have to wait too long before he could jerk himself off.

Rodney struggled beneath his tormentor. He could feel his cock sticking straight up, dribbling as the hot mouth moved down his body. Please God, just let it go a little bit further down... He was barely conscious of the cuffs biting into his wrists, of the rope around his ankles, even of the sock stuffed into his mouth. All of his attention seemed to be concentrated in his throbbing cock. The fact that he was being abused while tied and gagged and wearing his uniform receded into the background. He whimpered in relief as he felt warm air being exhaled upon his rigid dick. Oh yeah. This was it...it had to be. The mouth couldn't be far behind. His hair was plastered to his scalp with sweat, it was soaking into his open uniform shirt, and even the necktie bound around his eyes was wet with the perspiration running down his forehead. He felt the hot wetness flickering on the tip of his cock and shoved his hips upwards to get more of it. And then, nothing...

"Hey, Reggie, I have a great idea! Now that you've got this guy all hard, why don't we have the pig on the bed finish him off? That will really kill his career, one cop sucking off another one. What do you think?" Nick noticed that Reggie was panting, dark pools of sweat soaking through his shirt, and a wet spot forming in the crotch of his khakis. It looked as if old Reggie was having a good time, all thanks to Nick. Reggie muttered something under his breath, but Nick paid no attention. Since Officer Curran had taken care of him, he felt much calmer. Now he could concentrate on what was really important, the humiliation of Patrick Curran. He had another idea percolating in the back of his mind, but it would have to wait until they had the second cop up on the bed, shoving his hard dick down Curran's throat. Once that was over and done with, then they could implement the latest plan that was only half formulated in Nick's mind. It might be risky, but... it would be a perfect ending to the evening. Reggie tried to brush Nick away as he made a movement towards the cop lying trussed up on the floor, but Nick grabbed him by the shoulder, his fingers digging into the flesh. "Didn't you hear me? I said that I want film of this guy getting blown by Curran. Don't give me any trouble, Reggie. You're having fun here, all due to me. You can jerk off later."

Patrick had continued watching the abuse of his fellow officer. He was so horny he was bouncing on the bed, in the vain hope that somehow the movement would bring him off. He pulled once more on the ropes and cuffs binding him, but nothing gave. He moaned through the gag in his mouth. The wool socks that held the soaked bandana in his mouth had been tied very tight, and were cutting into the corners of his mouth. The fat knot at the back of his head was digging into his skull, especially when he let his head rest on the pillow. He became more alert as the guy with the camera, the creep who had raped his mouth, interrupted the fellow who was working over the cop on the floor. As he overheard their conversation, he became agitated. He really didn't want to be forced to suck his fellow officer's cock. He really didn't! He began trying to yell through his gag, and redoubled his efforts to get free. He strained every muscle in his body as he pulled on the cuffs holding his hands secure over his head. The brass bedstead shook and creaked, but it held firm. The masked captor who had been filming the scene turned towards him and laughed. "Hey, it looks like the big guy can't wait to suck some more cock. Let's make him happy."

Rodney heard the conversation between his two captors, and began moaning in consternation. So the guy tied to the bed really was a cop, and not someone dressed up in a cop uniform for kinky sex. He began rolling around on the floor in a vain attempt to get free. Sure he was horny, and desperate to cum, but to have another cop suck his cock! And to have it captured on film! No, this couldn't happen. He lashed out desperately with his bound feet. The guy who had been tormenting and teasing him had risen from Rodney's prone body, so he had more room to move. His struggling and kicking was in vain. He was picked up by the shoulders and feet, and dumped on the bed. He heard a grunt as he landed on the man bound to the bed. Oh boy...he could feel the hard erection of his fellow captive pressed against his stomach. And his own erection just wouldn't go down.

Through gritted teeth Reggie said "Let me do this. I'll get Curran to suck Graham's cock." "Sure, buddy, go ahead. Let's see how you do." Nick laughed. Reggie sounded really ticked, and judging from the bulge in his khakis he was as horny as hell. Nick was looking forward to capturing all of this on film. "But...let pig number two see what he's doing. That'll make it a lot more fun. Take off the blindfold. And let's put on his hat, too." Nick picked up Rodney's uniform hat, and placed it on the cop's head. Then he picked up Officer Curran's hat from where it had fallen on the pillows and clapped it on the hefty blond cop's head. "Just let me go ahead, OK? I can handle this. I know what I'm doing."

Reggie pulled Rodney upright, and with trembling fingers he loosened the knot of the navy blue uniform tie that had been used as a blindfold. It fell down around Rodney's neck, and he heard a muffled gasp from the cop. He wrapped one arm around Rodney's chest, while he slid the other arm between Rodney's legs and lifted him up until his knees were resting on Officer Curran's chest. Whew! This guy was a featherweight compared to Curran. He held the struggling cop tightly, his crotch pushed up against Rodney's ass. Oh shit, he was horny. He really, really had to cum. This was torture. He reached down and with some difficulty untied Rodney's ankles. He pushed Rodney up a bit further, and spread his legs. Peering over Rodney's shoulder, he could see that his stiff cock was positioned just above Curran's mouth. Reggie pulled down the socks that were tied around Curran's mouth, and sticking his fingers into his mouth, extracted the saliva soaked bandana. Before Curran could do more than gasp for breath, Reggie grasped Rodney's cock and, pushing him forward, stuffed the cop's erection into Patrick's mouth. Rodney tried to pull away, while Patrick attempted to move his head, but Reggie was relentless. He pushed his body up against Rodney, driving his crotch into the cop's meaty ass, forcing his body forward, forcing Rodney's hard cock further down Patrick's head. He reached around Rodney, and with one hand grabbed the back of Patrick's head, pulling it up. Keeping his body close to Rodney's, he pulled out his own stiff dick, and shoved it into Rodney's cuffed hands. "Pull on it. If you don't, it's going to go somewhere that you really don't want it to."

As Rodney's erection was plunged into the slick warmness of the booted cop tied on the bed, he tried to rear back, but resistance was futile. He looked down into the eyes of the man who was being forced to suck his cock. As the big blond guy's head was pushed into his crotch, he closed his eyes in shame. He didn't want this to be happening, but...it felt so GOOD! Then he felt something being shoved into his hands, secured behind him with his own handcuffs. He heard an order hissed into his ear. He wasn't sure what the threat implied, but he wasn't eager to find out. While the cop tied to the bed sucked on his cock, he started to jerk off the hard dick that was thrust into his cuffed hands. A rocking rhythm developed between the three of them. Rodney felt his cock starting to pulse. Aarrgh...oh God...this felt so good...it shouldn't but it did...more sweat broke out on his body... he bit down on the sock in his mouth...UNNHH UNNHHH...he shrieked through his gag as he exploded.

Reggie heard Rodney scream through his gag, and heard Patrick choking as Rodney shot his wad down the booted cop's throat. Rodney's hands had instinctively grabbed tighter on Reggie's cock as he shot. It was enough to send Reggie over the edge. He clutched Rodney tighter, resting his head on Rodney's shoulder, pressed against Rodney's sweat soaked uniform shirt, he bit down on the necktie that had been used to blindfold Rodney. Reggie chewed on the tie as he felt himself cumming, sweat pouring down his face as his semen spurted onto Rodney's fine ass, and trickled down the back of the cop's legs. Spasm after spasm wracked Reggie's body; he had been erect and ready to shoot for so long that it seemed as if the orgasm would never end. He released his grip on Patrick's head, allowing the mounted cop to pull his head away from Rodney's cock, and spit out what he could of the cum that had been deposited in his mouth.

Nick turned off the camcorder. He had everything on tape that he wanted; now he had something else to take care of. He couldn't believe it, but he had another erection. This one he decided to take care of himself; he had had another brilliant idea, one that would humiliate the second cop. He had enough on tape to finish off Curran; this action would be the icing on the cake of his hatred of cops. He pulled out his hard dick as he walked towards the bed where three men lay. Reggie was panting away, Officer Graham was grunting through his gag and Officer Curran just lay there like a log, moaning with cum dripping out of his mouth. Just to make sure he didn't make any noise, Nick shoved the wadded ball of bandana back into Curran's mouth, and pulled up the socks to keep it in. If everything worked according to plan, Curran would have another kind of gag in his mouth soon. Nick pulled Reggie off the bed. Old Reggie had a glazed look in his eyes, and made no protest. He then rolled Rodney off the bed, ignoring the grunt that came from the cop as he hit the floor. Nick needed to share that bed only with Curran. He straddled the cop's thighs, noting that Curran's cock was still waving in the air, hot and red. He could feel it through his jeans as he sat on Curran's upper thighs. The sight of the white rope biting into the cop's riding boots made him even hornier. Mmm. This was going to be fun. He wanted to get this over with as quickly as possible. Nick spat into his fist and started jerking on his cock. He felt the bound cop beneath him start to stir and moan. It was a bit too late for that. Nick felt his balls start to tighten up. Oh yeah. He raised himself up as he felt his cock start to spurt for the second time that evening. As his cum sprayed out of his cock, he directed it towards Curran's black boots. Hmmm, someone was going to have a clean up job. He sighed with satisfaction as he finished cumming. He tucked his penis back into his jeans, and got off the bed. Reggie was sitting on the floor with a goofy, satisfied look on his face. But Reggie wasn't the one that he was after. He grabbed Rodney by the shoulders, and dragged him to his feet. "Clean up time, cop!"

Rodney had been lying on the floor, trying to recover. He couldn't believe what had just happened to him. He had just come down the throat of another police officer! And...from the corner of his eye he had seen one of the thugs holding them captive filming the scene. He lay on the floor, his uniform trousers and his briefs puddled around his ankles. His jacket and shirt had fallen down to his cuffed wrists and his necktie was lying around his neck, still knotted. He could feel the cum that had been sprayed on him drying on his meaty ass and his thighs. Then he felt himself gripped by the shoulders and dragged upright. He heard the guy who been filming him say "Clean up time, cop" as the tape that had sealed his lips shut was ripped off. He coughed and spat out the sock that had been stuffed into his mouth. Oh, what a relief! Before he had time to savor the relief, he found himself being hauled up onto the bed, facing the high black boots that were now splattered with semen. "You've got a clean up job here, Officer Graham. Get to it!" Rodney felt hands grabbing his hair, forcing his head towards the boots. He struggled, but in vain, as his face was jammed against the boots, his face pushed into the cum. As the hands pulled on his hair, he reluctantly started licking. Hmmm, this didn't taste so bad after all...

Patrick lay cuffed to the bed, watching his hapless fellow officer being forced to lick criminal cum from his high black boots. He couldn't see too much, the light blue uniform shirt, it's back stained dark with sweat and navy blue jacket having fallen down around his companion's wrists, obscuring most of his ass and thighs. Patrick could see that the navy blue trousers and white briefs were tangled around the guy's ankles, his feet bracketing Patrick's thighs. If he twisted his head to one side, he could see Rodney lapping away at his boots, his head being held down to the boots by one of the masked men. Patrick's wrists were aching from being handcuffed to the bed's brass headboard, the cuffs biting into the flesh. If only he had his hands free, he knew what he would do to the bastards who had done this to him. And then, with one free hand...Patrick groaned into his stuffed mouth as he contemplated his dick, still hard and waiting for release. He had another taste in his mouth besides that of cotton. Why wouldn't his erection go down? After all the terrible things that had happened to him, why was he still hard and desperate to cum?

"That's enough, pig." Nick pulled on Rodney's hair and jerked his head up from the boots. "You fucking sick pervert, I'll..." Nick slapped his hand over Rodney's mouth, stifling his outburst. Hearing the cop mumbling under his hand gave him a physical thrill, which he ignored. He'd already got off twice tonight – he wasn't greedy! He laughed as Rodney struggled beneath him, and Officer Curran grunted impotently through his gag and rattled his cuffed hands on the brass headboard. "Hey, big guy, I see you've still got a woody. Don't worry, that's going to be taken care of soon. But first things first. Buddy, toss that tape up here. I've got to keep pig number two quiet for a bit longer."

Reggie was still sitting on the floor, in a bit of a daze. He couldn't remember the last time that he had cum with such force. He was fingering his cock, which had sprung to life once again, wondering whether he should have a second go at one of the cops. He still hadn't had the fun he wanted with the big guy. Did they have enough time for him to work over Curran one more time? The big guy just looked so sexy, lying there, cuffed and roped and gagged, his uniform half stripped from his body. Reggie thought about how he would like to have this guy tied up at home, with no worry about interruptions, and all the time in the world to work him over, and make him cum again and again...His pleasant reverie was broken by Nick's voice. Damn, this probably meant that it was time to go. They would tape up Officer Graham's mouth, and then leave. Reggie sighed and scrambled over the floor to where the roll of duct tape had been dropped, and threw it over to where Nick was holding the cop down on the bed.

Rodney writhed on the bed, trying to escape from Nick. He was hampered by the fact that he was partly lying on the big guy bound to the bed. Now that he was pushed down on the bed himself, the weight of his own body and that of the guy on top of him pressed down on his cuffed wrists. The pain was excruciating. He tried to kick out, but his uniform trousers and his briefs were tangled around his ankles, his feet just touching the floor. He watched as the guy on top of him ripped a piece of duct tape off the roll with his teeth, the other hand still clamped across Rodney's lips. That hand was removed for an instant, and then the long piece of tape was plastered across his mouth, preventing his cries for help from being heard more than a few feet away. Once his mouth was sealed, Rodney's captor ran his hand down Rodney's bare chest, over his stomach, until it came to rest on his groin. Rodney's cock was semi-hard, and he gritted his teeth and turned his head away as he felt the masked man starting to caress it. "Hmm, piglet is getting excited, is he? We'll have to see what we can do about that. But first, let's get that nice uniform of yours off. "

Nick undid Officer Graham's black shoes, dropping each one on the floor. The cop was trying to kick out, with little success. With his trousers around his ankles, his mobility was severely limited. The cop didn't sound too happy once he knew Nick's plan. Grunts of distress came from behind from his taped mouth, but with his hands cuffed behind his back there wasn't a great deal that he could do to hinder Nick. Once the shoes were off, Nick ran his fingers over the soles of Graham's feet. The black socks provided little protection. Nick sniggered as the cop squealed. This guy had sensitive feet. Sadistically, Nick moved his fingers over the cop's feet again. He liked hearing the cop shrieking through his gag. After playing with the feet for a few minutes, Nick grabbed the uniform trousers and the briefs, and yanked them off, letting them fall to the floor. He left the black socks on Rodney's feet. "Half the job done, now for the rest..."

Once his feet were free of the encumbrance of his trousers Rodney started kicking out in earnest. Now that he could see what he was doing, he had a chance of making contact with some flesh. The masked guy sniggered, stepped out of range, and then leaned over the bed and flipped Rodney on his stomach. Rodney felt his ankles grabbed and pulled together. Lying on his stomach, and with his hands cuffed behind him, he was no match for his captor. His ankles were crossed, and rope was wound tightly around them. In a minute his feet were secured. Then he felt hands slowly moving over the backs of his calves, and then higher. He tried to utter a protest through his taped mouth as the hands slid between his legs, caressing his inner thighs, and more. He jerked as fingers brushed his balls. His cock, now quite hard, was pushing against his belly. The hands withdrew, and he gave a sigh of relief until something cold and hard was pressed against his right temple. "I'm going to un-cuff your hands for a minute, but if you do anything stupid, you're going to regret it. Do you understand me? Shake your head if you do." Rodney had no choice but to nod his head in agreement. He wasn't stupid enough to struggle with the barrel of a gun pressed against his head. A hand fumbled with the cuff on his left wrist, and then it came loose. As he laid still, the gun still pressed against his head, his jacket and shirt were pulled over his hand. The action was repeated on his right hand. Now Rodney was clad only in his black socks and his white crew neck t-shirt, which was still pulled over his head, resting on his shoulders. What was going to happen now?

"What's going on? What are you doing?" Reggie had been watching Nick's actions with increasing unease. Why was he stripping the second cop? He thought that they would follow the original plan, changed somewhat by the introduction of the second cop. They would film the cop, and then leave him tied to the bed. He couldn't understand why Nick was removing Officer Graham's uniform, unless he wanted a souvenir. As Reggie thought about that, he liked the idea. Too bad it wouldn't fit him, but...perhaps he could pick up a couple of items. He had an idea as to why Nick wanted a genuine police uniform, but he didn't want to think about that. Reggie had a respectable and lucrative job, and he somewhat regretted getting involved in this scheme. But...it had been so incredibly sexy. If they got out of this without being caught he could relive it in his mind over and over again. Then Nick told him his plan, and Reggie's heart sank.

"We're going to dump these guys off in the parking lot of the cop shop. Chowing down on each other. Kinda maximum exposure, don't you think?" Nick asked. " Are you crazy? They must be looking for Curran! And Graham too by this time!" Reggie pleaded. "Relax, it's only a few blocks away, and I'll be driving the cruiser, dressed in uniform. I'll drop the pigs off with their friends, take off and you can pick me up." Nick laughed. Reggie was going to argue more, but he saw the manic gleam in Nick's eyes, and said nothing. Nick still had Graham's gun in his hand, and this time he knew that the bullets were still in the gun.

He groaned to himself, but kept his mouth shut.

Nick started removing his own clothes. Once he had stripped, he picked up Officer Graham's uniform shirt. "Whew, this pig sure has been sweating a lot. And sitting in traffic a lot, too." He slid the shirt on, and after buttoning it up he pulled on the navy blue trousers. "A bit loose, but they'll do." He did up the belt of the trousers and then buckled on the duty belt. He donned Graham's jacket, shrugging it over his shoulders. He picked up the hat from the bed and placed it on his head, and then, sitting down on the side of the bed, he put on Graham's shoes. "What do you think, buddy? Do I look like a cop? Oooops, one thing missing." Nick began unknotting the navy blue tie that was still hanging around Rodney's neck. "Yuck, this is kinda wet, too. These cops really do sweat like pigs, don't they? Ha ha ha." Nick fastened the collar of the uniform shirt, and placing the tie around his neck, knotted it. "Now we're ready for some more action."

Nick was feeling intoxicated. He was wearing the uniform of one the hated cops, and it felt great. He looked down on the figures sprawled on the bed. Graham, face down, wearing only his black socks, and his white tee shirt bunched up around his neck. Curran, with his breeches resting on the top of his boots, his shirt and jacket open, his tie hanging around his neck. The two cops were helpless, vulnerable. Nick felt a surge of power rushing through his body. He could do anything he wanted to with these cops. They were cuffed and tied and gagged, and couldn't do anything to stop him. He picked up Officer Graham's discarded briefs from the floor and draped them over Patrick's face. "Get a good sniff, pig. What they were holding is going to be in your mouth in just a few minutes." As he said this, his cock became hard as a rock. Wearing the cop uniform, with these two guys at his mercy, was a powerful aphrodisiac. He unzipped the fly of the stolen uniform trousers, and pulling his cock out of his boxers, he started jerking on it. Which one would satisfy him? He hadn't wanted to be greedy, but...He turned his head to look at Reggie, and saw that his partner in crime was now standing up, his cock jutting out of the fly of his khakis, and good old Reggie was jerking off like his life depended on it. "What are you waiting for buddy? There are two hot cop mouths waiting for us. Let's take advantage of them while we can."

Patrick shook his head, trying to dislodge the sweaty cop briefs that covered his nose and eyes. He couldn't help inhaling the odor. He raised his torso from the bed as much as his bound position allowed him to in an effort to remove the briefs. They slid farther down his face, over his gagged mouth. But his movement caused his uniform hat, which Nick had placed back on his head prior to him being forced to suck off Rodney, to slide off and it now lay on his face, obscuring his vision. As he tossed his head to get rid of it, he felt movement on the bed. The hat was removed from his face in time for Patrick to see a struggling and cursing Rodney being dragged off the bed by one of their captors, while the second was climbing on to the bed. Patrick recognized the khaki clad man as the one who had made him cum earlier. He tensed up, waiting for his gag to be removed. He had heard what the first guy had said about two hot cop mouths. This man had his cock out of his trousers, hard and dripping. Patrick closed his eyes and waited for the inevitable. Then he felt hands fumbling around the neck of his shirt. He opened his eyes to see the man straddling him holding a finger against the mouth of his mask, while Patrick's uniform tie dangled from the other hand. Then the tie was pulled taut in both hands and descended towards Patrick's face. It went over his eyes, and was knotted at the back of his head. He was now blindfolded. Only a little light penetrated beneath the tie. Hands started moving over his body.

Reggie couldn't stand the rubber mask any more. Sweat was pouring down his face and dripping down his neck. He had to get rid of it. But the cop must not see his face. He glanced over his shoulder to see Nick wrestling Rodney to the floor. As he turned back to look at Officer Curran, he saw that the bound cop's eyes were fixed on his face. He put his fingers to his lips, to indicate silence, and then pulled the cop's necktie from under the collar of his shirt. He blindfolded Curran and pulled off the mask with a sigh of relief. He didn't have to worry about Officer Graham seeing his face; he was sure that Nick was going to keep him fully occupied. He discarded the mask and started moving his hands over the big guy's chest, massaging it. As Curran started to moan Reggie's cock twitched. This was more his style! He moved his hands lower, kneading the soft flesh of Curran's belly. Leaning over he licked the sweat that was starting to pool in the hollow of the cop's throat. He savored the salty taste, and then began to move his mouth further down. The cop's nipples were erect, and became harder as Reggie used his tongue on them. As he slid his body further down the bed, he let his hands roam down over the hips, to the inside of the thighs. Curran uttered a stifled moan as Reggie's finger started stroking the flesh. And Reggie's cock jumped again. After the violence of his previous ejaculation, he hadn't expected that he would become so horny again in such a short period of time. But the thought of the things that he wanted to do to this big guy had kept intruding into his mind. With any luck, Nick would take his time with Officer Graham. Reggie moved further down the bed, and as he did so, he felt Curran's erection hit the underside of his chin. The cop lifted his hips, trying to maintain contact with the flesh. Boy, this guy was really horny. He must be desperate to cum! Reggie didn't want that, not yet. He wanted to cum first.

Nick dragged Rodney off the bed, forcing him to his knees. The cop's face was red, his eyes glaring at Nick as he uttered defiant curses from beneath his tape gag. This was good. It added to the fun. But...Nick noticed that his victim's cock was now at full mast, starting to dribble. He sniggered to himself as he pulled the nightstick from the duty belt. Rodney's eyes bulged in fear. Ha, the cop thought that he was going to be beaten. Nick had another use in mind for the nightstick. He moved it slowly down

Officer Graham's chest, until it rested in his groin, just next to the hard penis. Nick flicked the end of the cock with the nightstick. "Hey, it looks like you're enjoying this cop. You're all hard and leaking." He dropped the nightstick and grabbing Rodney's head, he pushed the cop's face into his own groin, rubbing it over the cloth of the uniform trousers. "How does it feel to see me wearing your uniform? It must be getting you hot, since your dick is so hard. Get a good sniff, since this is the last time you'll see your uniform. Now, I think it's time for the cop to have a little snack. Time to chow down on some beef sausage."

Rodney had fought as he was dragged off the bed. He looked up at his captor, dressed in his uniform, and was overcome by a wave of humiliation. The bastard was wearing HIS uniform, with his prick sticking out of it! He tried to swear at the creep, but his curses were stifled by the tape over his mouth. Then he saw the criminal pull out the nightstick. Shit! Was he going to be beaten to death! He relaxed slightly as it was rubbed against his chest, and then flinched when it flicked against the head of his dick. He closed his eyes and clenched his cuffed fists in impotent fury. Why the hell was he hard again? Then his face was crushed into the crotch of his captor. He could barely breathe as his nose was squashed against the fabric of his own uniform trousers. Then a hand grabbed his hair and jerked his head back. The duct tape that sealed his lips shut was brutally ripped from his mouth, and before he had time to protest, a hard cock was shoved into his mouth and down his throat. A hand on the back of his head kept it firmly in position, pressed against the navy blue cloth. He could hardly breathe, and the buckle of his duty belt dug into his forehead. He choked as the cock was rammed back and forth in his throat. Before long he heard the guy who was raping his mouth grunt and then sprays of cum were flying down his throat.

Patrick groaned into his spit-soaked gag. This guy was good. His hands and tongue were hitting all kinds of sensitive spots. If only he would make contact with his cock! He couldn't see what was going on, being blindfolded with his necktie. But he could feel his captor moving further and further down his body. It couldn't be long! He felt something brush up against the tip of his penis, and he pushed up his hips in an attempt to maintain the contact. He knew that he wouldn't need much...just a little rubbing, a little sucking and he would be over the edge. Then he felt the man straddling him move up his body and then...hands pulling down the socks tied around his mouth. The wretched saliva soaked bandana was removed from his mouth, replaced by...a big tongue. The guy was kissing him, shoving his tongue down Patrick's throat like another gag! Patrick then felt something hot and wet spray across his bared chest. Hmmm. Maybe now he could get some serious attention paid to his erection. Patrick moaned through his tongue gag, and thrust his hard cock up into the air, hoping that his captor would get the hint. The guy sagged down on Patrick's body, keeping his tongue in Patrick's mouth. This guy had a tongue like a cow!

Nick kept his cock in place for a minute or two after he had shot his load. Then he pulled it out and picked up the sodden white sock that had previously gagged Rodney. He grabbed Rodney's sodden hair and pulled his head back. "Open up, piglet. I've got to keep you quiet while I get your friend ready for your trip, and I wouldn't want you to wake up the neighbors. That wouldn't be very nice now, would it? "The cop tried to avoid the sock pressed against his lips, but some of the fight had gone out of him. Nick shoved the sock into his mouth, and then taped it in place. Then he turned towards the bed to get Curran ready, and nearly had a fit. There was Reggie sprawled on top of the cop, without his mask, and it looked like he had his tongue down the cop's throat. This was too much! He picked up the rubber Spiderman mask, and pulling Reggie off the cop, he snarled at him "Are you fucking crazy? Get the mask on and help me get big boy here ready for transport." He had slapped his free hand over Curran's mouth, stifling any outcry that the cuffed cop might try to make. While he did so he saw the cum spattered over the cop's chest, and noticed that the cop still had a big erection, his cock leaking pre-cum. Hehehehe. Too bad that he couldn't film the rest of the evening, but...Curran's cop friends would see the final act live! While Reggie pulled on the mask, Nick pushed the wet bandana back into Curran's mouth. Nick intended on replacing it with something else in just a couple of minutes, but he needed him silenced for the time being. Curran made no effort to keep out the gag, even when Nick pulled up the socks and pushed the knot between his teeth. He just made a pathetic moaning noise.

Reggie pulled on the mask, grinning sheepishly as he did so. He knew that it had been a stupid move, along with removing the cop's gag, but he was glad that he had. It had been so sexy grinding his tongue into Curran's mouth while he came all over his body. He really did wish that he could take the big cop home with him. He followed Nick's curt orders, holding an arm wrapped tight around the cop's neck while Nick unfastened one bracelet of the handcuffs from the brass headboard, and then proceeded to cuff the cop's hands behind his back. Letting the big man fall on the bed, Nick and Reggie untied his feet from the headboard and bound them together. The cop put up a perfunctory struggle, but his heart didn't seem to be in it. Then Reggie and Nick picked up Officer Graham and dumped him on the bed. Nick ripped off a strip of the duct tape and plastered it over Rodney's eyes. Nick and Reggie were going to have to take off their masks when they left the house, and they didn't want Graham to be able to identify them.

"Snack time, pigs! Sorry it won't be doughnuts, but I'm sure that you'll enjoy your treat just the same." Nick taunted the two policemen as he began to arrange their bodies on the bed. He and Reggie placed Officer Graham with his crotch over Officer Curran's mouth, and his head lying by Curran's hard dick. Nick pulled down the grey socks, removed the spit soaked bandana for a last time, and prying open Curran's lips, pushed the semi-hard cock into Curran's mouth. Nick took a piece of rope and wrapped it around Curran's neck and Graham's waist to keep the cock gag securely in place. Then he ripped the tape off Rodney's mouth and attempted to do the same thing. Rodney knew what was going to happen and put up much more of a struggle, half-strangling Patrick in the process. No way did he want to have another cock in his mouth especially that of a fellow police officer. He kept his lips tightly pressed together, even when Nick pulled on his hair. It was only when he heard Patrick choking and felt his teeth biting down on his own cock because of his struggling that he opened his mouth. Rodney choked himself as Patrick's rock hard penis was shoved down his throat. Even as his head was being roped to Patrick's body, he could feel the mounted policeman moving his hips, trying to get his cock further down Rodney's throat.

Patrick groaned as he felt his erection being slid into the mouth of his fellow captive. He hated himself as he tried to maneuver his cock further down. Even as he did so, he felt the cock in his own mouth start to grow. Hmmm. This was an interesting development. As the two cuffed and bound men were lifted from the bed and carried outside Patrick passed the point of no return. The bouncing was enough to cause him to shoot down the throat of the man he was tied to – there was nothing that he could do to stop himself, bound and helpless as he was.

Nick and Reggie staggered under their load as they carried the two bound cops outside to Officer Graham's cruiser. Reggie thanked God for the dense shrubbery that bordered the driveway. No one would be able to see them except from the foot of the driveway, and on this quiet dead end, inhabited mainly by elderly retired people, it was most unlikely that anyone would be out for a late night stroll. Reggie was sweating from fear as well as from exertion. Why couldn't they just leave the two cops in the house? What if Graham had been reported missing, and the cops were looking for his cruiser? Nick swore under his breath as he managed to get the rear door of the cruiser open. "Geez, these guys' aren't featherweights, are they? OK, you know where the police station is located. Park on Fairmount, around the corner. I'll dump these two off in front and then drive around the corner and dump the car. Be ready to take off and head towards Bloor."

Nick hopped into the driver's seat and pulled out of the driveway, waiting for Reggie to get out and go ahead of him. He pulled off the mask and then placed the uniform hat on his head. He looked at himself in the mirror as he listened to the two men in the seat behind moaning. Hmmm. He looked quite convincing dressed as a cop. It had been such a turn on forcing Officer Graham to service him while he had been wearing the cop's own uniform. The moaning in the backseat increased in intensity. It sounded like someone back there was having a good time. He wondered which one it was. Curran had looked as if he could have popped at the slightest touch. But...he didn't care. All he had to do was to reach the police station undetected. He followed Reggie out of the cul-de-sac, and turned onto Park. Only four blocks to go. Three. Two. One. There was the police station! Nick stopped outside, leaving the motor running, and jumping out of the car, he opened the rear door of the cruiser. He pulled out the two cops, and dumped them on the sidewalk. He hopped back into the cruiser and took off, rounding the corner. There was Reggie waiting for him! He jumped out of the cruiser and got into the waiting car. "We did it buddy, we did it!"

THE REVENGE OF MY ALL MALE STAFF

Written by: Timmy Backman

Being the only Straight male in my department puts me in constant conflict with the gay guys I supervise. And my obvious straight status had always caused my subordinates to view my disciplinary actions as being gay bashing.

None-the-less, because business has typically been perceived as a straight male bastion, these guys delight in teasing me, and conniving to put me down...to take revenge for my perceived gay bashing. But, they don't do anything that would require more than a reprimand. If I were a better man, I'd have left long ago. But, I'm security conscious, and afraid to seek new employment. Besides, my brother is the president of the company and he tends to look after me.

There is one member of the board that I don't get along with at all, Myra. She and I have clashed on many occasions and we are always trying to one up the other. Well, I think she may have finally put together a plan that would result in my demise. Unbeknownst to me, she had won the hearts of my totally gay male department and together, they had devised this devilish plan to humiliate me.

So, my department was required to make a presentation to the board at the end of the month. With that in mind I had made assignments to my immediate staff to develop strategic portions of the presentation, which I would then coordinate, direct and lead in the production. We are in the fashion industry and our company produces and sells men's fashions and accessories. Because this is the fashion industry, the fact that I am straight makes me more of the "odd man" out. My gay charges fit right in.

My department is tasked with new trends and developments in the industry and fashion world. I had thought that my direction and planning had gone well and that the final presentation would be a feather in my cap. Little did I know that Myra and my staff were conspiring to make me look foolish in front of the entire company fashion board.

At the meeting, I introduced my staff and gave a brief background of our work and how each young man would cover a specific area of new innovations and trends in men's fashions. First I introduced Terry, a rather cute (for a guy), smallish young blonde guy, to tell us about men's hair care. Terry thanked me and proceeded into his discussion of men's hair products. He came to a hair mousse product and wanted to demonstrate the product (which was not originally part of our planned presentation). And he asked me to be his demonstrator, or guinea pig, if you would. I declined, saying that it really wasn't necessary. But Terry insisted to the point that the board agreed and asked me to relent. So, I stepped forward as two of my other subordinates rolled out a small barber type chair. First, under the auspices of making me comfortable and not soiling my suit, Terry took my suit jacket and then winking at the snickering board he tugged, pulled and removed my tie. This made me feel a little undressed in front of the board, from the corporate environment sense. I mean, what's an executive without his suit jacket and tie for crying out loud? A few moments later I was seated in the barbers chair...

Then around me went the typical barbers bib. With the smirk of an evil scientist, Terry snapped on a pair of latex gloves like he was going to give me a rectal exam, which he would have probably relished. Now, he started describing the mousse and he liberally applied it to my hair and scalp, rubbing and massaging and making a general mess of my hair. Although it felt very pleasant to have my scalp massaged, I felt self-conscious having this young man make a mess of my hair in front of our board. But, what I didn't know was that this new hair mousse incorporated a relaxing agent that was absorbed through the scalp, and Terry squeezed on another big glob and worked it feverishly into my scalp. Of course, since he was wearing latex gloves, none of the mousse came in contact with his skin. So, he felt none of the effects. Terry droned on as he continued to massage my hair and scalp. He actually giggled as he felt me relax beneath his fingertips.

Although not a patch, this mousse uses the same principle of absorbing through the skin and apparently, it didn't take this stuff long to begin to work. My eyelids grew heavy and I was struggling to keep them open. Terry startled me when he pinched me on the cheek and informed me that he was through and that I should continue with the rest of the presentation. Still not aware of what was happening to me; I groggily shook my head and rose from the barber chair, with the bib still around my neck. Also, if I could have seen myself in a mirror, I would have been mortified at what he had done to my hair. Terry had spiked it in several places, making me look something like a disheveled punk rocker.

The board just looked at me a bit in disbelief. As I started to continue, Terry came back apologetically and removed the bib, with a jerk, much like a magician would snatch a tablecloth off a table without destroying the dishes. Now I was back to just my suit pants and open neck dress shirt with no tie. Myra, my nemesis on the board, just sat there confidently stifling a giggle.

So, continuing with grooming, I introduced Bob, who was to introduce men's cosmetics. I was about to return to my seat when Bob took me by the arm informing me that he also needed a demonstrator. I again declined, but the chairman of the board gave me this uncooperative glare, so I quickly changed my tune. Holding me by my arm Bob directed me to the front of the room.

Bob talked about how men with light complexions will want to have a tanned appearance year round, and the newer lotions provided a quick solution, as he too snapped on a pair of latex gloves. With this he began to apply some to the backs of my hands, then my face. Once Bob had covered my face with the lotion, he moved down to my neck and attempted to go lower. When he got to this point two of the other fellows came out and took my arms and unbuttoned my cuffs while Bob made quick work of my remaining shirt buttons. As I protested the other two quickly pulled my shirt from my pants and made short work of pulling the shirt from my upper body. Quick as a wink, Bob was again talking and applying tanning lotion. So, these three guys had managed to remove my shirt against my feeble protests, leaving me bare above the waist.

Now, what I didn't know about the lotion Bob was applying to me was it also had an additive. However, the additive to this tanning lotion was akin to Viagra. So, while I was being relaxed by the solution in the hair mousse, my sexual drive was being stimulated by the additive in the tanning lotion. At the same time, Bob's expert hands were moving around my upper body, massaging my chest stomach and back. The way he was working on me was most stimulating. I don't know about you, but the relaxing feel of a massage is very sexual...even if applied by someone of the same sex.

So, there I stood; my moussed hair spiked, me beginning to feel like I'd just taken my third shot of whisky, with no shirt on and this young man rubbing all over my upper body in a very suggestive manner. I was really, really relaxed, but, my dick was beginning to stiffen; both from the lotion additive and from Bob's expert handiwork. As my dick stiffened, it began to create a tent in the front of my pleated suit pants. The hair mousse had me a bit confused, and the growing tent in my pants was causing me embarrassment, but the board seemed to be amused at my predicament.

Then, in my intoxicated state, I made some stupid statement about my legs not having a tan. Well, that just played into the guy's hands. Bob grinned and winked at the board, and especially Myra, as he stated that legs need to be tanned too. At the same time he squatted in front of me and quickly worked on my belt and zipper. In my subdued state, I didn't block his actions, but just peered down at him with a dumb look on my face and simply watched Bob attack my belt and slacks.

Once Bob had stripped my belt from their loops and had unbuttoned and unzipped my pants, he allowed them to drop and crumple into a heap at my feet, leaving me in just my white boxers, shoes and socks. Then ignoring my feeble protests, he raised each foot and pulled my pants from each leg. By this time, there were considerable snickers, both from the board and from the rest of the guys on my staff who had gathered close by to assist Bob. My pants were snatched away by one of the guys and disappeared from site, just like my coat, shirt and tie had.

Then I felt an incredible sensation as Bob began applying tanning lotion to my legs. Not only did he massage the lotion in with his palms and fingers, but, in a playful manner, he would rake my legs with his manicured fingernails, even though they were encased in latex gloves. This caused me to giggle and flinch at the tickling sensation, and it caused my dick to stiffen even more. Also, when he got to my upper thighs, Bob would run a lotion covered hand up my boxer leg, tweaking my ass or bumping my balls. I grinned stupidly at the board as I was handled and lotioned.

By now, my dick was producing a sizable tent in my under shorts, creating a large gap at the leg openings. Bob's tickling, tweaking and bumping was causing my dick to twitch and grow even more. Even though aroused by the sexual stimulant in the tanning oil along with Bob's sensual, tickling massage, I was somewhat oblivious to my now obviously embarrassing state of near nakedness and sexual arousal. I was not even aware of the wet spot forming on my under shorts from the pre-cum oozing from my dick. I should remind you at this time that I am straight and not interested in the least in other guys...sexually. So, under normal circumstances, my situation, my condition would have been totally avoidable and rejected by me. But, the continued mind numbing affect of the hair cream and the sexually stimulating tanning lotion had me off guard, unaware, and sexually peaking at the hands of other men, guys, my guys, the guys that work for me. And, even though I was unaware, my guys were keenly aware of my condition and doing their dead level best to increase my humiliating situation.

The board was caught between being aghast at my performance and breaking out in sidesplitting laughter, especially Myra, who felt like she would soon be rid of me, because my brother would never be able to protect me from this lewd demonstration.

While the hair mousse continued to dull my mental capacities, the Viagra loaded tanning cream was doing a number on my number one sex gland and sending more and more blood to my pulsating dick. Plus, it was not just Bob that was massaging this sex stimulant cream all over my body, all the guys had donned latex gloves and joined Bob in this sexual massage and I was now being rubbed everywhere. Nearing unconsciousness, I was pushed back into the barber's chair, where they presented their Coups De Grass.

While the group of guys pushed me back to the barber's chair and out of sight of the board, one of the guys pulled the waistband of my under pants out as far as he could and one of the other guys dusted an ample dose of itching powder into my shorts making sure that my dick and balls had an ample coating. The itching powder didn't have an immediate effect, so I was oblivious to their action.

With me seated in the barber's chair, Bob continued to ramble on saying that it wouldn't be right to have tan legs and white feet. So, with help from his conspirators and with evil grins all around, they lifted my legs and off came my shoes and socks. Once I was barefoot, they took delight in rubbing my feet with tanning lotion. They even applied it to my wrinkled soles, which tickled like hell and caused me to begin to guffaw with laughter. I was a giggling, sputtering sexual mess. And everyone was really enjoying my predicament.

Not long after the foot tickling, the itching powder began to work on my hot, sweaty, pulsating crotch. Everyone else was laughing and giggling at me, but I soon stopped laughing and became extremely quiet. As the itching sensation increased, I began to resemble a cartoon-like character; my eyes grew wide as saucers and my mouth formed the proverbial oooooooh ring. My hips were twitching and bucking in the chair at the unbelievable itching in my crotch. I would have jumped up from the chair, but I was being held down. Soon everyone became aware of my silence and got very still and attentive to my situation.

Being held down in the chair with my feet up in the air, my only movement was in my hips. During this comical jerking action, two of the guys began again to stroke the soles of my naked feet. Well, I was itching and sexually excited and now again, I was being tickled beyond belief. I laughed and hollered like a maniac. Then there were some feathers produced and the guys holding me down began using feathers on my face, neck, legs and chest. Once they had me totally out of control and laughing and gyrating they let me go. Well, I sprang from the chair and ripped off my under shorts in order to get to the source of the incredible itching.

So, there I stood, or danced, completely naked and scratching at my lily white, itching crotch with my incredible erection bouncing in the air. I scratched and pulled and stroked trying to get relief from the itching...and then to top off my humiliation...my nuts tightened up and I had a mind shattering orgasm. I spewed cum and moaned and spewed cum and laughed and spewed cum and fell back into the chair...unconscious.

I guess Myra won that one because the meeting was videotaped. I have a copy and I still go back and whack off when I view it. My brother was in fact able to save my job, to Myra's chagrin. I did get an incredible reprimand, but when the ingredients to the lotions were discovered I was forgiven. My guys pleaded innocent and claimed that they had no knowledge of the extra ingredients in the hair mousse and tanning lotion so they didn't lose their jobs either.

In the end, my staff had gained their revenge for what they

had always perceived as my anti-gay stance. And I was not about to retaliate against them. But, I make sure to watch out for them now. And because of those memories and that video, these are the only guys that get a twitch out of my dick when I'm around them.

TIMMY GETS REVENGE, OR DOES HE...HMMM?

Written by: Timmy Backman and added onto by: Christopher Trevor

Timmy Backman was just leaving the Antonio Robinosky motivational seminar...and he was pumped. The speaker that had hosted the seminar was inspiring in so many ways, most of all on the subject on not being taken advantage of and not allowing others to use you to fulfill their selfish needs. During that part of the seminar Timmy Backman really paid rapt attention. Timmy, happily married to the beautiful, sexy Stephanie, they had one son, Timmy Junior. Timmy was a highly successful attorney and banking wizard and financier. He had also *constantly* been the subject, no, the word was victim that was the word the speaker of the seminar had stressed never allowing yourself to become, a victim. And sadly Timmy had been a constant victim of brutal tickle torture episodes plus teasing, edging and orgasm control. Well, at this point in time Timmy no longer saw being captured as playful, he no longer saw being tied up and tickle tortured as fun, fun maybe for the person doing it to him, but not fun for him as he himself laughed his fool head off while in the throes of forced sexual stimulation. To say it plainly, the handsome laddy (as he is many times referred to by his various tickle nemesis's and of course the author who is simply in lust for Timmy, Christopher Trevor) was sick of it. And Antonio Robinosky's seminar had just motivated Timmy to take control and eliminate all that tickling, teasing, edging and sexual control that he had been subjected to. In fact, the laddy was so motivated that he was beginning to plan to get some revenge for all the suffering he had done in the past, revenge for all the times he had become a tickle villain's plaything. What better way to get out from under all of this than to make the ones who had tickled tortured him receive the same kind of treatment themselves? And Timmy Backman decided then and there that he would start with Ronald, *Ronald Greene,* his supposedly best buddy in the whole world, HA!, the guy who had started all this. Ronald, who had tickled and teased Timmy the most with his heinous and villainous tickle inventions, Ronald, who had had the audacity to even abduct poor Timmy right from his own home in the middle of the night and then held him as a tickle captive for three days straight. Timmy thought how he would also deal with the likes of Valerie, the sexy villainess who had used the "Spinning Chinaman" numerous times to tickle poor Timmy and humiliate him in front of his wife. The "Spinning Chinaman", an art deco piece of furniture that Timmy had been duped and cajoled into purchasing and the thing now resided in his home. A giant wheel that could house a man his size, a party enhancer, wherein the recipient of the thing is strapped in and spun senseless...and in Timmy's case, spun senseless and tickle tortured in between. The game was always a question and answer game. If you guessed the answer to the question put to you, you were not spun and tickled. Poor Timmy however was spun and tickled whether he got the answer correct or not when questioned. Valerie made sure of that, and woe of woes, embarrassments of embarrassments, to be stripped to his socks and underwear and spun and tickled in the strapped up position in the device in front of his wife, horror of horrors. And all of it Valerie's doing... And then there was Douglas who would also get his share of revenge, Mr. Long Wang and his sexy but vixen-like assistant Makya Leakalot...and then there was Bull, Bull, the leather clad bartender who had turned the tables on ticklish Timmy at the leather bar and then even captured him and made him into the main ingredient in a huge salad at a fund raiser, talk about humiliating and being edged. Timmy thought of course of the Hong Kong tailor and of all people, his own brother Bruce. The handsome banker realized he had a lot of revenge to dish out...but, he was going to start with Ronald.

Timmy knew that Ronald liked to sit around in the late evening watching TV or sex videos. It was something that Ronald had bragged to his buddy about when it was just them hanging out every once in a while at Timmy's house while Stephanie and Timmy Junior were away at Stephanie's mother's house. While sipping beers and watching football games with Timmy Ronald bragged about his lonely evenings watching porn. So, with that in mind Timmy planned to use his military training, and in a daring commando raid-like fashion Timmy decided that he would secretly break into Ronald's house, subdue him and put the evil tickling Ronald through some of the same paces that he had subjected him to, or maybe even worse Timmy thought while sneering to himself. So Timmy, banker, lawyer and reserve soldier began to train himself for this self appointed mission. The guy already worked out and ran on a daily basis, but now he upped his exercise regimen and broke out his marshal arts guise, a black attack style outfit that would help him sneak up on unsuspecting Ronald. Timmy's outfit was his black pajamas style with black sash pants, he used his black OTC dress socks under the black ninja style shoes and he also had black gloves and a ninja hood that covered his head and neck with only a slot for his eyes. He decided he would black his face around his eyes so that the whites of them were the only part of his costume that was not the color of night.

After several weeks of planning, hard training and rehearsal, all in secret of course Timmy was ready and raring to make his assault on Ronald's house and the tickle madman himself. He knew that Ronald would be home this Friday, home and sitting in front of his TV. And on this night Timmy would finally get his revenge on Ronald and end his own ticklish victimization.

That Friday night Timmy told Stephanie that he had a special Reserve military weekend to attend to and that he would be gone the whole time. Timmy was planning on working Ronald tickle-wise all weekend, just as he had done to him that first time, a whole three days of being relentlessly tickle tortured. He planned to show Ronald no mercy. So, at around ten PM that Friday evening Timmy kissed Stephanie goodnight and left the house clad in his uniform with his duffel bag. Once out of the house he found a secluded place where he could change into his ninja/commando outfit and to black his face around his eyes. Once done he made his way to Ronald's neighborhood, driving as quickly as possible, not wanting to be seen in his guise, and slipped into Ronald's backyard.

The neighborhood was quiet and so was the house, but Timmy knew that Ronald was home. He snuck around and peered into several windows. Timmy was able to use his glass cutter to remove a pane on a window and then reach in and unlock the window itself. Then, it was just a matter of opening and slipping inside via the window, silently.

Once in the house Timmy was able to hear the sound of Ronald's TV blaring in another room. The laddy tiptoed to that door and peered in. And there was Ronald, sitting in his easy chair all relaxed with his feet up on the ottoman and behold, Ronald's feet were clad in thin black socks, HA, HA, and he was watching a video of Timmy himself being tickled and teased in one of his devilish devices. Timmy saw himself naked, tied down tight, with his cock sticking well up into the air and Ronald dancing around his naked spread-eagle body whipping him with feathers while a mechanical thing-um-a-jig tickled his tied down naked tootsies. The predominant sound coming from the TV was the screaming laughter of Timmy himself along with his breathless pleas for Ronald to stop. As awful as this was, Timmy immediately sprung a full erection in his ninja style pants. His cock poked out like a boy scout's tent pole on the fourth of July. After a moment or so of being mesmerized by the images on the TV Timmy pressed his erection down and almost painfully between his legs. He then secured the black rope clipped to his black sash and prepared to drop the lasso around his tickling nemesis Ronald; he would tie Ronald's ass up tight, strip the guy and put him through his own tickling paces, and see just how much he enjoyed being made to laugh till he was crazy with it.

Just about at the time that Timmy was going to lasso Ronald he spotted his nemesis's can of knockout spray.

"Ah, ha!" Timmy said to himself. "I can use that on Ronald like he used it and chloroform on me, and I can deal with him while he's unconscious."

So Timmy quietly picked up the can of knockout spray and slipped quietly up behind Ronald's chair. Timmy could still hear his own screaming and laughter on the video as he prepared to give Ronald a dose of his own sadistic medicine. Timmy wondered during which of his tickle captures the video had been made.

Timmy was about to spray Ronald in the face from behind when he heard the guy speak, "Welcome Timmy, welcome to my web, my spider's web that is, not my website, ha, ha. Jeez, but you just don't get enough of my special treatment. You have come here on your own this time, I didn't have to cajole or shanghai you this time, heh, heh, heh for you my laddy.'

Timmy was appalled at this speech...

Ronald had not moved yet, but he was addressing Timmy. Timmy could not figure out how Ronald knew he was there, he hadn't even worn any scents like cologne or body sprays. But a generous spraying from the can he had snagged and none of Ronald's knowledge of his presence would matter. Timmy quickly got in close to Ronald and he pointed the can at his buddy's face. Ronald did not seem to be surprised or shocked by this turning of the tables. With no hesitation whatsoever Timmy's finger pressed down on the can's cap, the can hissed loudly and the knockout spray sent a huge cloud of mist right toward the nose and mouth... but there was only one problem, the nose and mouth was Timmy's own, the can was spraying in reverse. Timmy was so shocked he didn't release the plunger, but kept spraying, and because he was shocked he was caught in at the point of inhaling large quantities of the stinking mist. Timmy's vision began to blur. He could still hear his own laughter echoing from the TV video...and he also heard Ronald laughing, as his ninja disguised body sank to the carpet. He dropped the can of knockout spray and he could see his tickle nemesis standing over him. In his stupor Timmy heard and saw Ronald laughing.

"Oh, what has happened to me?" Timmy asked himself as sleep claimed him. "Has Ronald captured me again? Have I once more fallen into his clutches?"

...and everything went as black as his ninja disguise...

"I must say my laddy you made it very easy for me this time," Ronald said as he took the protective gas mask away from his nose and mouth and crouched down next to his buddy, smiling maniacally. "And just look at this outfit you're wearing. Whatever did you have in mind for me?"

As Ronald snickered Timmy opened his eyes halfway and clenched his teeth...

"Ba-bastard you are Ronald," Timmy whispered and Ronald held up the spray can of knockout gas.

"One good whiff deserves another my laddy," Ronald teased and turned the can properly.

The hissing sound was all Timmy heard again as he inhaled and fell deeper into the arms of slumber...

"OHHHHHHH..." Timmy whimpered then as Ronald lifted him from the floor and carried him over his shoulder to another room...

"And may I say that your timing was perfect Timmy, just in time to try out my new gizmos as I call them," Ronald chuckled. "I haven't named them yet but I'm sure that that creative mind of yours will come up with something...when you see them that is... hardy, har and har for you once more my laddy..."

Ronald set Timmy down on his back on a long cushioned and spindle type table...He took the laddy's ninja outfit off him and used a wet cloth to de-black Timmy's face...

When Timmy came to a while later he was aghast at the twisted turn of events and the horrid irony he had suffered yet again. Wearing just his OTC black nylon socks he found himself stretched out on his back on a cushioned table. As his vision cleared and he looked around he saw that he was strapped down tight, no way of taking his revenge now. Like he had been on the video that Ronald had been watching when he'd turned the tables on him and captured him yet again Timmy's cock was flagpole hard and twitching, pointing straight up at heaven. Oh why oh why was it that when the things that he hated the most happened to him did his cock react by springing to full mast and betraying him?

"OHHHHH, oh man, oh my word, what, what in the hell happened?" Timmy asked as he squirmed miserably under the tight and binding straps.

"Some reserve soldier you are Timmy my laddy," Ronald said from across the room where he was standing at a table that was masked by a wooden partition attached to it.

"Ronald, you bastard, how did you know man?" Timmy grunted, lifted his head up and looked at his stretched out strapped down muscular body. "Oh fuck me, stripped to my danged socks yet again..."

"Like the boy scouts say Timmy, always be prepared," Ronald laughed and walked over to the table where Timmy lay, wheeling the other, partitioned table with him. "I've had that can of knockout spray set in reverse for the longest time. I always knew that if you somehow got the gumption to try to turn the tables on me that you would go for that spray can, and boy howdy I was right laddy."

Timmy simply grimaced angrily at Ronald as the guy set up the partitioned table next to his and then gave one of his socked toes a squeeze and jiggle.

"Now tell me Timmy, how many guys sit and watch TV with a can of knockout spray right next to them?" Ronald asked.

"I knew that that setup would be too much for you to resist."

"Ronald, you un-tether me right now, I did not come here to be tormented and tickle tortured by you again," Timmy steamed, his head up off the table again.

"No? And where do you usually go my laddy?" Ronald laughed and moved behind his partitioned table.

Timmy saw that Ronald had his underpants sticking out of his back pocket, jeez, just another trophy that the guy had snagged from him Timmy thought miserably as he lay there helpless and stripped.

"Ronald, listen to me man, Stephanie knows where I am, and she'll send the cops and..." Timmy began but Ronald held up a hand, silencing the poor guy.

"Timmy, Timmy, Timmy, I know you too well my laddy," Ronald said and took Timmy's chin in hand, pushing his head back down on the table.

Then, still holding Timmy by the chin Ronald leaned in close and practically whispered in the strapped down guy's face, "While you were sleeping off the knockout gas you dosed yourself with I called Stephanie and asked to speak to you. She told me that you had gone off on a military reserve assignment..."

Timmy's eyes opened wide in horror...and Ronald leaned in closer to his captured prey...

"And she told me you would be gone all weekend," Ronald whispered, sneering in Timmy's face, his lips close enough to kiss Timmy's. "So the way I see it, you came here with a plan to capture and tickle torture *me* bud. And you planned to keep at it all weekend..."

"Ronald, please..." Timmy whimpered his lips grazing Ronald's as he whispered out his words of pleading.

With a maniacal looking smile on his face Ronald pecked Timmy on the mouth, let go of his chin and stood up straight.

"Ronald, I made a mistake, please, please don't do what I think you're going to do..." Timmy panted and Ronald held up the accursed can of knockout spray. "Oh no, oh my word..."

Once more Ronald dosed Timmy and the poor laddy listened to Ronald's insane sounding laughter...

"Ronald, oh my! Oh my word let me off this thing!" Timmy bantered a short while later as the table he was tethered to spun at the speed of an old record player set on the 33RPM mode of action.

Timmy was now blindfolded as well as strapped down as he was being spun round and round...

"Oh lord, what's the point of this Ronald?" Timmy squabbled, twisting his blindfolded face from side to side. "I feel like I'm in a laying down position on Valerie's device called the "Spinning Chinaman."

"Just prepping you for the fun to come my laddy," Timmy heard Ronald say. "When you see the tickle devices I have in store for you to get this party going you're not going to believe it. They're my latest creation..."

"And made with me in mind I'm sure," Timmy went on as he spun round and round, his cock sticking up long, beefy and hard, pre cum oozing from the wide sexy slit of it.

"So have you accepted your weekend fate Timmy? And have you come to terms with the fact that your little ploy did not pan out as you intended it?" Ronald asked as he sidled up to Timmy as he spun and spun.

"What choice do I have Ronald?" Timmy garbled miserably.

A half hour to forty five minutes later Timmy was dizzied and disoriented as Ronald stopped the table spinning and whipped the blindfold off his captured prize...

Timmy looked around and around in his dizzied befuddled state and then up at Ronald as he stood over him, holding two square devices in his hands.

"And now Timmy, to get this tickle weekend started right these are what I plan to tickle that muscular body of yours with," Ronald said, leering down at the strapped down tickle captive. What Ronald was holding in his hands were two (although Timmy saw more of them on the table beside his, the table that was no longer partition blocked off) square metal boxes, each of them about the size of a Rubik's cube. On the bottom of the boxes was what looked like two-way heavy-duty adhesive tape and on the top of the boxes, sticking out of them...to Timmy's horror, a long stiff looking feather.

"Ronald, you can't be serious, you plan to keep me here all weekend?" Timmy asked, looking with dread at the two square boxes that his so called buddy was holding.

"Why not? You planned on tickling *me* all weekend," Ronald said. "Now, let me show you how these new inventions of mine work..."

"I'm not stupid Ronald, I can tell how they work," Timmy said throatily.

"We'll start with your nebulous nipples, how's that grab

you bud?" Ronald teased Timmy and then pressed the heavy-duty taped bottoms of the square boxes against Timmy's torso skin, just under where his nipple tips were jutted up and real juicy looking.

"It, it grabs me real tight man," Timmy responded and struggled to no avail under the tight binding straps.

Timmy watched as Ronald then moved the tips of the feathers attached to the boxes against his nipple tips.

"Oh my," the poor laddy whispered and lay his head back, his lips quivering. "No wonder you took my danged underpants off me... I don't need three guesses to know where another of those boxes is going..."

"And I'll be taking your pretty black socks off you too bud," Ronald quipped as he stepped to the foot of the table and started slowly peeling Timmy's OTC socks off him. "I want you to get the full thrust of being tickled this time my pal of pals. No silky socks to protect these beautiful feet of yours from my feathers this time. This time we're going for the beef and gusto..."

"Oh fuck, oh woe is me..." Timmy whispered as his feet were bared...

Soon, there were square boxes scattered over Timmy's strapped down body, all of them set at his most ticklish spots, the feathers pointed and pressed against those ticklish spots.

When Ronald was done he looked over his work...

At the sides of Timmy's strapped down bare feet were two boxes set at each foot, so that four feathers were pressed against the bottoms of Timmy's meaty and wrinkled tootsies. Having his feet tickled was horror enough but what Ronald had done with the other boxes filled the poor boy with even more dread...

There were boxes adhered to his thighs, the feathers pressed against his inner thighs, ready to tickle the thick ticklish skin there...

At his sides were two boxes, their feathers stretched and pressed against the tip of his cum oozing hard cock. Ronald had tied a good length of thin rope around Timmy's balls, to insure that the laddy stayed hard for his tickle ordeal...

At the sides of Timmy's stomach region four boxes were set up, two on each side of him, the feathers all pressed against his washboard abs. A fifth feather was pressed inside the ticklish guy's bellybutton, one of the worst spots that anyone could be tickled...

Just under his broad shoulders was a box each, the feathers embedded in his armpits...

As Timmy lay there feeling like a sacrificial lamb of sorts Ronald was setting up the final two boxes on the sides of Timmy's neck, the feathers pressed against Timmy's big bull sized collar area...

"Ronald, don't do this to me man, all these feathers, I'll laugh myself into insanity here," Timmy pleaded.

"And then some my laddy, and then some," Ronald said breathlessly and quickly tied the blindfold back over Timmy's eyes. "You'll spin and laugh atop that table my laddy of lads, and that's just the warm-up for what I have planned for you this weekend..."

Timmy squirmed in misery as the table started rotating yet again...

"Oh no, Ronald, no, no..." Timmy called out.

Unknown to Timmy because he was now blindfolded Ronald held up the remote control device that would turn the feathers spinning in their square boxes on...

"And away we go my handsome laddy..." Ronald said and pressed the first button on the remote control.

Timmy pressed his lips tightly together as he felt the tips of the feathers pressed against his nipples come to rotating life.

"OH NO, no," Timmy hemmed and tried again to suppress his laughter, to no avail. "HA, ha, ha, ha, ha, and away I go to laugh city, spinning round and round I go..."

Ronald chuckled and pressed another button on his remote control...

Timmy huffed and hawed as the feathers against the sides of his neck came to spinning life...

"HAH, HAH, HAH, HAH, HAH, Ronald you bastard, y-you're ticklin' my danged neck!" Timmy reeled. "This is no way to treat a buddy you call your laddy!"

"Ah but Timmy, it's the best way to treat a buddy I call my laddy who's devilishly ticklish," Ronald responded.

Ronald smiled evilly and pressed yet another button on his remote control...

Timmy then grinned behind his blindfold, started sweating as he was spun like a record and screamed out, "Oh no, not my pits, oh my poor pits!" as the feathers embedded under his arms came to life. The feathers at his armpits didn't rotate so much as they buzzed and vibrated against the tender skin there. Timmy hunched his broad shoulders up a bit but it didn't do a thing to alleviate the ticklish sensations consuming his armpits...

"HAHAHAHAHAHA!" Timmy screeched and when Ronald turned on the feather that was pressed into Timmy's belly button the poor ticklish guy felt like he could bolt off the table... good thing he was strapped down tight... "OH Ronald, this, THIS, was not how it was supposed to be tonight! HAHAHAHA! Oh my word, that feather ticklin' my danged belly button is murder, pure murder!"

Timmy lifted his head up off the table, grinned insanely behind his blindfold, clenched his teeth, spittle laughed and laid his head back down...

Ronald moved around Timmy's spinning table and pressed another two buttons on his remote control, bringing the four boxes situated around Timmy's stomach area to life...

The four feathers started spinning their tips against Timmy's stomach area, sending the poor trapped guy into louder guiles of laughter...

"OHHHHHHHH, HAHAHAHAHA, what a ticklin' I'm getting this time!" Timmy laughed. "All these feathers, all these goddamned feathers..."

"Now Timmy for the moment I'll bypass that juicy cock of yours and instead set the feathers at your inner thighs in motion," Ronald said to Timmy as the guy spun and spun atop the table.

"Jeez, thanks for small favors bud, HAHAHAHAHA!" Timmy responded but then found himself in even deeper throes of laughter as the feathers at inner his thighs came to spinning life. "YAHHHHHHHHHHHH!"

"What are friends for after all Timmy?" Ronald chuckled. "We're almost there now, almost done with getting all my boxes turned on and the feathers spinning..."

"Dang, I feel like the record of an old fashioned record player here, HAHAHAHAHA," Timmy screeched miserably. "The way I'm bein' spun and those feathers pressing against me sure does attest to that Ronald..."

"Brilliant my laddy, I knew you would come up with a good idea for a name for my latest tickle invention," Ronald quipped and with a maniacal looking grin on his face pressed another button on his remote control.

As Timmy said, "Yeah, the record player tickler machine," his words were suddenly and dreadfully cut off as the two feathers at each of his naked feet came to life.

"OOOOOHHHHH PWWWAHHHH!" Timmy laughed like a loon. "HAHAHAHAHAHAHA OH DANG, not my feet Ronald, not my feet, oh please, not my goddamned feet..."

Timmy spun and the feathers at his feet seemed the worst of all the tickling that he was presently being subjected to. They moved and glided over and over the meaty bottoms of Timmy's big feet, slid over his heels, along his arches and just under his toes...

"And now for the crème de la crème Timmy my laddy," Ronald said and pressed the final button on his remote control.

To Timmy's dismay and forced ecstasy the feathers aimed at his cock tip came to rotating and tickling life...

The poor guy could no longer speak as he simply laughed and laughed and laughed...

The feathers tickled his cock tip and snaked down the sides of his erect and pulsating shaft. Timmy oozed droplets upon droplets of pre cum as his cock was tickle tortured.

Watching intently Ronald felt his own cock stiffening in his pants as his good buddy laughed and spun...

"Ah Timmy, what a weekend its going to be my laddy," Ronald said and Timmy tried to plead through his laughter but it was no use, he just could not speak. "I think a good couple of hours of what you're enduring now will be a good warm-up for what I have at my tickle palace..."

"HAW, HAW, HAW, HAW, HAW, HAW, HAW, HAW, NOOOOOOOO, HAW, HAW, HAW, HAW, HAW!" Timmy screamed wildly.

"Oh yes Timmy, oh yes, tomorrow morning we'll be on our way there, and just think bud, Stephanie thinks you're away at a military reserve weekend," Ronald said fiendishly.

As the feathers at his cock slid to his sweaty balls Timmy oozed more droplets of pre cum. The need to shoot his load was setting in hot and heavy but in his heart of tickled hearts Timmy knew that it would be a while in coming that Ronald afforded him that pleasure...

As Timmy laughed he thought miserably of how his plan for revenge had gone belly-up, and so had he as he lay there being tickled...and on his up belly at that too the poor boy punned to himself...

And now, had Ronald said that he would be taking him to his tickle palace come the next day? That would be Saturday... and Timmy knew that once Ronald had him at his tickle palace he would be tickle relentless with him... God knew how many new tickle inventions Ronald had acquired at this point...

"Oh my word, what have I done?" Timmy asked himself. "I told Stephanie I was going to a military reserve weekend...but being captured and tickled and now kidnapped to Ronald's tickle palace sure didn't figure in that equation..."

As Timmy spun atop the table and laughed his head off and sweated he thought how the next two days were going to seem an eternity...

The sounds of his laughter began to sound like sputtering as the night wore on...and on...and on...

THE MVP

Written by: Christopher Trevor

When I was in college I was on the football team. Actually, I was the best fucking player Dale College had that year and because of me they won most of the games and the national championship. When I graduated I was given a special award for being the MVP of the football team. What I want to tell you about happened when we won the national championship. Medford College was our opponent team and they had come to play on our field. I was merciless throughout the game and we won, making Dale College the champion football team that year. After the game was over and we had whooped it up on the field two of my best buddies lifted me up on their shoulders and carried me off the field...all the way to the locker room. As I was carried like a king I took off my shoulder pads and dropped them on the floor outside the locker room. In the locker room my two buddies put me down and we all doused each other with endless bottles of champagne. Standing by my locker I stripped out of my football uniform down to my white calf length sweat socks, my white briefs and my football uniform tee shirt. As I stood there about to take off my tee shirt I heard my name being called by the whole team.

"Brian! Brian! Brian!" they all chanted together, sounding like cavemen in the musty and man scented locker room.

I smiled as my two best buddies came over to me and again lifted me to their shoulders. They carried me to the center of the locker room where most of the team was waiting, all with a bottle of champagne in their hands. I was about to be thoroughly doused. I whooped along with them as my buddies held me tightly on their shoulders. Then, the team all opened their bottles of shaken up champagne and pointed them at me. I was doused and squirted with champagne till I was drenched with it.

"WHOOOOOO!" I roared happily.

"MVP! MVP! MVP!" the team hooted.

I pulled my tee shirt off, baring my muscular chest and tossed it into the crowd of my screaming teammates. Someone caught it and I heard him say he was going to keep it as a souvenir.

"Hey bud, that's my shirt, not some damned trophy!" I called out with a wide lady-killer smile.

A few of the players doused my huge bare chest with champagne and from behind me I received some congratulatory slaps on the ass. When I got to be too heavy my two buddies put me down on the floor and they each opened their bottles of champagne. They poured the contents of the champagne bottles over my head and even soaked my damned briefs with the stuff, pouring it over them.

"WHOOOOO!" I screamed out happily. "Celebrate you fucking guys, fucking celebrate!"

When the champagne was done I was sitting by my locker catching my breath as all the other players got dressed. I sat there in my briefs and sweat socks, smiling, savoring the feeling of being MVP. A while later my two best buddies came over to me. They, like me were still not dressed, both of them wearing just their briefs.

"Hey you two..." I said.

"Here's your smelly tee shirt," Dennis said to me and dropped my tee shirt in my lap. "Clark caught it when you threw it."

"Yeah, we caught the fucking guy sniffing it," Vinny added jokingly.

I smiled and took a big sniff of my sweaty smelling tee shirt.

"I can see why," I said jokingly and tossed the tee shirt into my open locker.

I stood up and looked at my two best buddies.

"I cannot believe we've won the national championship guys," I said, holding out my hand.

Dennis shook my hand followed by Vinny.

"Hey man, we couldn't have done it without you..." Dennis said and gave one of my jutted up nipples a squeeze.

"Yeah, you are the MVP man," Vinny said and with a smirk on his face squeezed my other nipple.

"Hey you two, easy with those titties..." I said jokingly.

"You don't like to have your big tits squeezed Brian?" Vinny asked me and squeezed my nipple again. "I refuse to believe that all those gorgeous girls you date don't go after these big ol' tits of yours..."

Then, before I knew it they were laughing and joking as I tried to prevent my two buddies from squeezing my nipples. It became like a wrestling contest. At one point Vinny managed to get my arms pulled behind me. He held me tightly as Dennis amused himself squeezing and teasing my nipples till I yelled out in pain.

"OWWWWW! You fucking tit squeezer!" I roared at Dennis with a sly looking smile on my face.

Vinny let go of my arms and I turned around to attack him but then it was Dennis' turn. He grabbed my arms in a tight grip and held them tightly behind me as Vinny took his turn squeezing and twisting my now aching nipples real hard. Again I yelled out loudly in pain. I struggled in Dennis' grasp as Vinny squeezed my nipples like crazy.

"YOWWWWW!" I screamed loudly, trying to smile through it all. "C'mon you two, give me a break here!"

Then, Dennis let go of me and Vinny stopped squeezing the bejesus out of my nipples.

"Shit guys that hurt..." I said, rubbing a hand over one of my sore nipples.

"Yeah, but I bet we can make those big juicy titties of yours feel a lot better MVP," Dennis said, smiling fiendishly at me.

"What in the fuck do you two have in mind?" I asked him

in reply.

"Well, judging from the pre-cumming hard-on in your smelly briefs it sure as all hell looks like you enjoyed having your big titties tortured," Dennis said to me.

I looked down, and sure enough, I was hard as a fucking rock and pre-cumming in my briefs. I looked back up at my two buddies.

"Shit guys, I got that hard-on from winning the game and being carried off the field," I said defensively. "No fucking way I was getting off on you two torturing my damned nips."

"Let's find out..." Vinny suggested and took a step toward me.

"Look guys, I don't know what the fuck you have in mind but..." I began to say, but then Vinny leaned down and slurped one of my big nipples into his mouth. "OHHHHHHH, shit! Hey man, what're you doing? OH GAWD, that feels fucking great..."

He gently held my nipple between his lips and tongued it.

"OHHHHH man, yeah..." I found myself crooning.

Dennis stood beside Vinny and took my other nipple into his mouth. He treated it the same way Vinny was treating the other nipple he had in his mouth.

"Oh fuck yeah, work my titties you guys..." I sighed.

I propped my back against a locker and caressed the backs of my two buddies' necks as they slurped, sucked, and bit on my nipples.

"OHHHHH..." I crooned loudly. "Fucking tit hungry guys you two are. What's the matter, your girlfriends don't let you suck their tits?"

As they worked my nipples they ran their hands over my big pecs, squeezed my hips, and snapped the elastic in my briefs.

"You know guys I'm getting all sorts of ideas here..." I said breathlessly. "OOOOOO, yeah, slurp those nips of mine, work on them..."

A while later they stopped and we all looked at each other and we all had rage hard-ons in our briefs. There was no denying we all loved what was happening here, kinky and strange as it was.

"What sort of ideas are you getting?" Dennis asked me and gave one of my very erect nipples a fast squeeze.

"Stand at attention and I'll tell you..." I said, taking on an air of command and feeling the need for some revenge here, seeing as I had just been their plaything.

Dennis and Vinny looked at each other, shrugged, and snapped to attention. They looked great standing there rigidly at attention wearing nothing but their damned briefs. I stepped in front of them.

"So you boys want to worship my football player body, is that what this is all about?" I asked them and ran a hand over my chest.

"Yeah, you could say that MVP..." Dennis replied.

I pretended to consider his reply and then turned my back on them, giving them a good view of my sexy rear. I could feel their eyes pulling my briefs down. My plan for revenge was working, plus I would get off my rocks.

"What if I wanted you guys to service me on other areas of my body?" I asked them. "Would you do it?"

I turned back around facing them and they said that they would, calling me MVP again. I nodded and told them that my armpits were real sweaty and tangy smelling from the game, giving them a sniff each.

"My armpits are downright fucking raunchy guys, they need a good cleaning," I said to them with a look of disgust on my face. "Do you two think you can service my pits till they're good and clean?"

They looked at each other and then looked at me.

"We sure as fuck could MVP, but first we want another go at those nipples of yours," Dennis replied. "They sure look tasty."

Before I could stop them they each had one of my nipples in their mouth again. This time they sucked them hard, squeezing my buns at the same time through my briefs.

"AAARRRRRR!" I cried out in pain and pleasure at the same time, realizing how they were somehow countering my little plot for revenge.

When they stopped working my nipples I leaned back against the locker, crossed my arms behind my head, exposing my hairy smelly armpits, and told my buddies to get to work. They stood on either side of me and began slowly tonguing my rancid armpits.

"MMMMM, yeah, lick those pits of mine..." I crooned,

enjoying being back in command.

They ran their hands over my stomach as they picked up the pace of licking and sucking on my juicy armpits. When Vinny's hand went near my sore nipples I told him to back off.

"No touching my damned tits for a while!" I barked. "First one that tries it I'll fucking tie his hands behind him."

They licked my armpits faster and even kissed them. They sucked my armpit hair into their mouths and scoffed on it like it was a cock, sucking the juice out of it. They ran their tongues over the sides of my pits and then with the tips of their tongues they went back to the center of my armpits. A while later I ordered them to stop and to resume standing at attention. They did as they were told. I sniffed my armpits.

"Damn, you guys did a good fucking job, I guess you two are good for something after all," I said to them and gave them each a hard slap on the ass. "My pits smell good and freshly clean."

"Thank you MVP," they said in unison.

"Now guys, I have another treat for you," I said, looking down at my sweaty wet briefs. "My damned briefs are funky like you would not fucking believe. Between the sweating I did during the game and the champagne bath they were given before they smell real rank and probably taste like pure unadulterated raunch. Not to mention the fact that I trickled piss and pre cum in 'em..."

I gave the elastic waistband of my briefs a pull and let it snap against my skin.

"You two kinky bastards think you're up to the challenge of cleaning my damned briefs?" I asked them.

"We sure would like the challenge you hot MVP," Dennis said anxiously.

Again I pretended to consider his response and then ordered them to get busy servicing my briefs.

"Sure thing MVP," Vinny responded. "But you know what we want first...again..."

"Oh no, no..." I said softly as their mouths went after my sore tits. "OHHHHHHHH!"

They held my arms tightly behind me and slurped hard on my nipples, bighting on them with their front-most teeth.

"Fucking tit hungry bastards you two are!" I ranted. "Fucking should have tied your hands behind you when I said I would...AARRRRR!"

Some revenge I was getting here huh? After a long while they stopped working my nipples and then kneeled down at my sides. They held me by my tree-trunks like thighs, running their mangy hands up and down my legs as they began slowly licking my moist briefs.

"OOOOOHHH yeah, tongue my briefs you two perverts!" I demanded, running the palm of my hands over my sore nipples.

They sucked on the sides of my briefs, licked my throbbing hard-on through the thin cotton material, and even ran their tongues underneath them, licking my big plum-sized balls too.

"OHHHHHH yeah, yeah, feels fucking great..." I crooned. "SOOOO fucking good..."

They turned me around and licked and sucked the back of

my briefs, strumming their hands over my tight hot buns at the same time. I wiggled my ass seductively and leaned against the locker, my stinging nipples pressed against the cold metal. They snapped the elastic in my briefs against my buns and continued licking them.

"Fuck guys, I'm goin' crazy here..." I said breathlessly. "Never thought I could get off on this kinky shit you're dishing out on me..."

They turned me back around and looked up at me, pleading in their eyes.

"Go for it..." I whispered.

Together, they pulled my briefs down and off me. My hard throbbing cock stared them in the face, dripping and oozing pre-cum. Vinny went first. He gobbled my thick veined cock into his mouth and began sucking on it as Dennis toyed with my smelly sweat socks, rolling them up and down.

"Oh yeah, suck my big meat, eat that cock," I groaned.

I leaned against the locker with my hands up behind my head again. Vinny stopped sucking my cock and Dennis took his turn, slurping my big tube steak into his mouth. Vinny lapped at my balls, tongue bathing the fuck out of them, sending chills through me.

"OH fuck yeah," I gasped. "You fuckers..."

I pulled myself to my tiptoes and goose bumps broke out all over me as they serviced my cock and balls, driving me into a frenzy. I roared in ecstasy like a caged animal. As they went on and on servicing my cock and balls they yanked their cocks out of their briefs and began jacking off at the same time.

"Oh yeah, stroke those cocks you guys, yeah, get off with me," I sputtered.

After a while longer we all shot potent and hefty loads. Vinny and Dennis shot their loads onto my feet and when I came Vinny had my cock in his mouth so he had the pleasure of swallowing and scoffing down my pearly juices. We all moaned and groaned in ecstasy as we shot our man juices. When we were done I watched in awe as Vinny and Dennis licked their cum off my smelly sweat socks.

"Oh yeah, lick my feet you two," I said as I caught my breath, satisfied now that I had gotten my due where these two tit hungry bastards were concerned.

Moments later they finished licking their cum off my socks. They stood up and gave each of my nipples a fast lick each.

"Man, that was fucking unbelievable," I said to Dennis and Vinny. "You suppose this makes us fags?"

"Nah, just real hot," Dennis quipped, squeezing one of my nipples.

We all smiled at each other. Later, after we had showered and gotten dressed we all left the locker room. After graduation from college I never saw Dennis or Vinny again but every once in a while I think about my two kinky friends and what we did that day and I still get a hard-on.

ABOUT THE EDITOR

Christopher Trevor

Christopher Trevor was born in July 1963 and grew up in New York City. As soon as he was old enough to know how he began writing fiction and has been writing gay erotic/fetish stories for the past ten to twelve years at this point. He became an avid reader as well from the time he knew how and reads everything from fiction, to non-fiction to biographies of interesting and unusual people, people who have made a difference or who have paved the way for others. Christopher attributes his writing artistic inspiration to artists  such as Etienne, Tom of Finland, Tagame, The Hun, and most notably Joe T, who Christopher has had the pleasure of speaking with and even meeting over the last few years. Christopher states, "Joe T encouraged me to write about my fetish because I was embarrassed about it at the time. Joe T said that when we are embarrassed about something that makes it even more enticing somehow." Christopher totally agreed and never stopped writing in this genre. Erotic writers who inspired Christopher Trevor were: Tom Shaw (author of "That Day at the Quarry), C.S. White (author of Big Sur), Larry Townsend (author of countless erotic novels), and Mason Powell (author of the classic story "The Brig.")

Christopher discovered that not only did he enjoy writing erotic tales but that after his first bondage experience he had a genuine flair for it. Writing to erotic oriented magazines about his first bondage experience truly opened the floodgates for Christopher where this style of writing is concerned. Christopher thanks the handsome and muscular "Greg" for that experience way back in time. Christopher took "Creative Writing" courses every semester during his high school years and while other friends of his stopped writing what they loved to write about as time went on Christopher never let a day go by when he didn't write something... "I feel that if I don't write every day I will die," Christopher has said many times over.

Foot fetish stories and all things related; spanking fetish, erotic shaving, muscle bondage, tickle torture, and hardcore stories are just a few of the areas of gay eroticism that Christopher enjoys writing about and inspiring in others as well. As one internet buddy said to Christopher where the black socks fetish is concerned, "Until I started talking with you I never gave a thought to my socks when I got dressed for work in the morning. Now when I pull my dress socks on every morning I get a chill up my spine."

Christopher is proud of the erotic effect he has on people...

Christopher Trevor is also the author of:

The Executive Guide to Foot Fetishism and Office Discipline
   1-887895-36-1

Executive Ties That Bind
   1-887895-37-X

Don't! Stop! That Tickles!
   1-887895-31-0

The Taming of Dominick
   1-887895-45-0

Timmy and The Hong Kong Tailor
   1-887895-30-2

Love, Torture and Redemption
   1-887895-32-9

Timmys Ticklish Trials
   978-1-887895-74-3

The Gym Instructor
   978-1-887895-44-6

Milked
   978-1-887895-66-8

Erotic Street Blues
   978-1-887895-97-2

The Abusive Wager
   978-1-887895-04-0

Terry's Appointment and Other Tickling Stories
   978-1-934625-08-8

The Military File
   978-1-934625-21-7

Quirks
   978-1-934625-24-8

Timmy and the Evil Dr. Vonvellicator

978-1-934625-42-2

Blackmail

978-1-934625-47-7

Tickled Kink

978-1-934625-49-1

Humiliation

978-1-934625-58-3

Discipline

978-1-934625-07-1

Look for them where you bought this book, Amazon.com or
TheNazcaPlainsCorp.com

www.ingramcontent.com/pod-product-compliance
Lightning Source LLC
Chambersburg PA
CBHW070816250626
47170CB00006B/2124